After

FRANCIS CHALIFOUR

TUNDRA BOOKS

Published in Canada by Tundra Books,
481 University Avenue, Toronto, Ontario M5G 2E9

Published in the United States by Tundra Books of Northern New York,
P.O. Box 1030, Plattsburgh, New York 12901

Library of Congress Control Number: 2004117246

Library and Archives Canada Cataloguing in Publicat

Chalifour, Francis
    After / Francis Chalifour.

ISBN 0-88776-705-2

    I. Title.

PS8555.H2758A75 2005   jC813'.6   C2004-90414

ONTARIO ARTS COUNCIL
CONSEIL DES ARTS DE L'ONTARIO

We acknowledge the financial support of the Government of Canada
through the Book Publishing Industry Development Program (BPIDP)
and that of the Government of Ontario through the Ontario Media
Development Corporation's Ontario Book Initiative. We further
acknowledge the support of the Canada Council for the Arts and the
Ontario Arts Council for our publishing program.

Printed and bound in Canada

This book is printed on acid-free paper that is 100% recycled,
ancient-forest friendly (40% post-consumer recycled).

1 2 3 4 5 6   10 09 08 07 06 05

If you've lost someone close, this book is for you.
You know what I am talking about.

In memory of a friend and actor,
Stéphane Pominville,
who taught me
how to enjoy every second on stage.

To my mother,
who taught me
how to make my bed and how to love.

To Marc and Luc, my mentors,
who taught me
how to use utensils properly.

PREFACE

Be careful. Nothing lasts forever.
> – The old lady with whom I shared
> my turkey sandwich on the bus.

I've always thought that a big laugh is a really loud noise
from the soul saying, "Ain't that the truth."
> – Quincy Jones

I thought I would never survive it. How do you survive something you think is all your fault? If only I had shoveled the snow when my father asked me to, or walked the dog when he told me to, or kept my room as neat as a ship's cabin like he wanted me to. If only I had been a better son. I went as deeply into the darkness as it is possible to go. But I climbed back into the light. I survived, and this is my story.

1 | SHOCK

Though the June night was hot, my hands were icy as I fumbled for my keys at the front door. Mr. Enrique, my Spanish teacher, leaned out of his car window. "Good luck, son," he yelled as he drove off down the dark street.

My mother opened the creaky wooden door just as I turned the key.

"Maman, what's wrong?" I asked.

She looked ashen, numb. "It's over. *Point final.*" When my mother says *point final*, everybody snaps to attention, even the dog, so I didn't resist when she took my arm and led me to her bedroom. It was the only place in the house where there was an air conditioner, though it hadn't been turned on since my father had lost his job. The stairs felt like they would never end. No stairway to heaven, that's for sure. My mother closed the bedroom door very carefully behind her as if the sky – or the air conditioner – might fall on me.

"I have bad news, sweetheart." Her blue eyes were blurry with tears.

Sweetheart. The last time I could remember her calling me that was when we were both crammed into a toilet cubicle in the ladies' room at Eaton's because I was too young to go by myself and she was coaxing me to hurry.

I sat down on the big rumpled bed, feeling like Louis XVI waiting to go to the guillotine, or Louis Riel waiting to be hanged.

✻

1992. I hate that year. Queen Elizabeth described it as an *annus horribilus* because Windsor Castle burned down and Charles and Diana separated. That was the year that George Bush got sick on a visit to Japan and vomited on the Japanese Prime Minister. Serbs in Bosnia-Herzegovina declared their own republic. What else? In June my father hanged himself in the attic.

✻

After that, the world did not stop, although that seemed odd to me at the time. Here's the short version of what happened after.

Summer: I spent the summer more or less in my room with the curtains drawn. When it got too hot, I took my guitar out on the stairway that runs down the back of our house, where nobody could see me. My Aunt Sophie took charge of my little brother, Luc. I think they went to the park or the swimming pool or to the doughnut shop a lot. I can't say for sure, because I didn't notice. My mother left the house every morning and went to work at the post office. When she got home she scrubbed every possible surface in the house, and when she was finished she started scrubbing all over again. After days of whining to be let out and then whining some more to be let back in, our dog, Sputnik, spent a lot of time under the porch asleep.

Autumn: I went back to school. Luc went to kindergarten in the mornings and to day care at the church down the street in the afternoons. When he was home, he stuck to my side like a burr. Maman worked, scrubbed, and yelled at me, Luc, and the dog.

Winter: You should know that Montréal in winter is cold and dark and snowy. We were three strangers living side by side in an old house on a steep street. Christmas came and went. Maman's scrubbing lost momentum, and she spent a lot of time staring at the fire in the fireplace. By January the street had grown so narrow from snowdrifts and buried parked cars that I felt like an Arctic explorer when I made the trek home from school. Luc wanted me to carry him whenever we were outside. He was so heavy in his snowsuit and boots that I thought my back would break.

Spring: I had my sixteenth birthday. Maman got a better job. Luc talked to Sputnik as they played catch in the backyard. The darkness receded.

~~~

I think that about wraps up the nuts and bolts, but as I said, I can't be 100 percent sure. My heart lived a different, terrible life of its own that year. Time stretched and shrank and grief took up residence inside me. It was a living, breathing creature that I could not control. This isn't the story of what I did that year. It's the story of what I felt.

~~~

I was on a school trip to New York with fifteen other kids and three teachers. I was wild to go, but because money was so tight at home, I made a deal with the principal that I'd help the caretaker for a half hour every day. For months I'd mopped the halls and emptied trash cans and pried gum off desks, but I got to New York.

We had a lot lined up: visits to Rockefeller Center and Times Square and the Metropolitan Museum to see the gigantic Temple of Dendur set up in one of the rooms. That was strange: this ancient building that human hands like mine had made over two thousand years ago and thousands of miles away, standing quietly in a museum while vendors hawked pretzels and hot dogs outside. I bought a souvenir for my father, a Rangers jersey. The Rangers were his favorite hockey team, after the Montréal Canadiens. He hated the Toronto Maple Leafs.

New York was great, but I was homesick. I love Montréal as if it all belongs to me, personally: it's my Olympic Stadium, my smoked meat sandwiches, my old brick house halfway up its narrow, tree-lined street, my friends, my music. I missed Luc, even though he woke me up at dawn every day to play with his Lego and Hot Wheels, not something I'd recommend as a quiet way to ease into the day.

***

The telephone rang in the hotel room. We were on the tenth floor but we could hear the buzz of morning traffic through the open window.

"Hey, Francis, it's your mother," Houston was sprawled on the slippery nylon bedspread flipping through a guide to the city. I had been flossing my teeth, something not to be skipped, especially when you've just eaten three hot dogs with sauerkraut, and you haven't brushed your teeth for three days in a row. Gross. I thought Maman might be calling because she was missing me, or she was worried that I was too hot or too cold or something. My mother is a champion worrier.

"Francis, you have to come back to Montréal as soon as you can," she said. "Mr. Enrique will drive you."

"Did Grandpa have a heart attack?" A month doesn't go by without a Grandpa Heart Attack Scare. I'm trying to make it sound funny, but it's not.

"Just come home," said Maman.

"Is Luc okay?" Luc is constantly swallowing his toys. That may sound funny too, but it's not. It must really hurt to swallow a miniature car.

"Luc is fine. I'll be waiting for you. I love you."

She hung up. I don't know why it didn't occur to me to worry, but I didn't. I simply pulled my backpack out of the closet and packed my U2 and Jacques Brel CDs, and the camera that my mother had given me for my last birthday. I'd had to rescue it from Aunt Sophie who threatened to throw it away when I took a picture of her on Christmas Day barfing on our molting green shag living room rug.

Mr. Enrique is, to say the least, an eccentric driver. He is also the weirdest man on earth. All the way to Montréal, he talked about his blind cat, Rococo. He told me that he would eat a human being before he'd eat his cat. Some choice. I don't remember much else about the drive – just Rococo and Mr. Enrique and the only Spanish phrases that I could remember, *¡Dos cervezas por favor!* with the upside down exclamation mark – very hard to find on a keyboard, by the way.

Your father is dead. That four-word sentence, spoken in my mother's soft, flat voice, changed my life forever. Mine. Hers. My brother's. My father had died. DIED in red capital letters, as enormous as the billboards on Times Square. No, bigger, more excessive, than anything I had seen in New York. A nuclear bomb exploding in my chest. Ten thousand guillotines chopping off ten thousand heads with a terrifying metallic clamor. The Space Shuttle Challenger disintegrating in flames in the sky over Texas. An electric shock pulsing through my veins and bones. My mind skittered around for some place to hide from the pain. There was nowhere.

That year was full of surprises and this was the first: sorrow hurts like hell. I swear my heart stopped beating. My throat constricted, and my belly hurt as if a wolf had eaten my guts.

I felt like a computer that had gone haywire, with images crazily chasing one another across the screen. My father would never wrestle with me again on the disgusting green living room rug that hid Cheerios and dog hair and the odd coin in its shaggy tufts. We wouldn't stuff ourselves with Smarties and jelly beans and then play hand after hand of poker on Sunday afternoons. He wouldn't pretend to be mad when he told me to turn off the lights in my bedroom after midnight when I was reading Superman comics. We would never watch hockey on TV on Saturday nights, slumped together on the old brown couch, eating popcorn.

I heard myself bawl from deep in my soul, if there's such a thing as a soul. My mother gathered me in her arms. I had almost forgotten the warmth they had once given me. When you are fifteen, you don't do this kind of thing anymore. I wanted her to hold me forever.

2 | ANGER

When I woke up the next morning, everything seemed the same for a moment. I was in my own room lying on familiar faded cowboy-patterned sheets in a bed with a headboard like a ship's wheel. The walls were as dry and cool as a wintry Arctic desert. I looked at the ceiling, freshly painted, thinking of an infinite white sea. I wanted to dive into it, not to drown so much as to freeze in it, to freeze time.

My guitar was leaning against the wall. It was a Christmas present from my father. He had taught me three songs that first day. My desk was in its usual place under a shelf of books neatly arranged by theme. The desk had belonged to my father when he was a kid and his initials were carved into one corner. I had cleared off all my junk from school before I left for New York. The only thing on it was a photo of Papa and me, grinning at the camera with a big bowl of candy in front us, holding our poker hands to our chests. I remember when Aunt Sophie took it. Maman had just cleared Sunday lunch from the table – an old table made from pine and Luc was singing to himself as he played with plastic margarine tubs on the kitchen floor. There was a pot on the floor, because the bathroom pipe was leaking water through the ceiling. I must have been twelve years old.

～

The first thing that hit me was a wave of guilt so enormous that I thought I would die too. Why did I leave my father for that damned trip? I knew Papa had been depressed since he'd lost his job a couple of years ago. He'd started working on the boats before his sixteenth birthday and he loved the sea and the broad St. Lawrence. One day he was loading cargo on a slippery deck when he wrecked his back. Two operations didn't help much. He must have tried to get hired on again at least a thousand times, but people told him he was too old and that the work was too hard. That was the beginning of the end. He was never the same after he lost that job. As far as my father was concerned, a man who couldn't work wasn't a man.

～

It wasn't as if we'd had no warning. At breakfast on a stifling June day last year, Maman announced that she and Aunt Sophie were going shopping, and that Luc was coming with them. "You're such a big boy now, *mon cher*." She pushed his hair off his forehead. "You need big-boy clothes for the summer." He looked unconvinced. She headed off a tantrum with a promise of ice cream when they were finished and turned to Papa.

"Ben, why don't you come with us?"

"Darling, you've asked me a hundred times. I'll be fine here. You know I hate shopping." Papa didn't look up from his crossword puzzle.

"Francis, you'll come right home from school?" She gave me a worried look.

"Sure." I knew she didn't want Papa to be alone.

Anyway, Papa was on his own that day. When I got home I found him lying on the cracked linoleum with an empty glass of milk and the vial for his pain pills beside him. There was a piece of paper on the kitchen table, held down by the salt shaker as if it might fly away:

Sorry. I'm going somewhere better. I'm fed up with my life.

I felt like he had slapped my face. My hands shook as I dialed 911. I knelt down beside him while we waited for the ambulance and turned his face to me.

"How could you, Papa?"

He tried to answer but he sounded drunk, as if he had a big potato in his mouth. It must have been the effect of the pills. I couldn't understand him at all. After eight minutes and ten seconds, the ambulance came, and they took him to the hospital. They told me that he was going to be fine, that he was a lucky man because I had found him. Not to worry. But I did.

I worried about him from that moment on, and I guess I'll never stop worrying, even though he's dead and beyond pain.

After I found Papa lying on the floor, I promised myself that I would never let him out of my sight again. All that summer, I followed him everywhere. When he was taking a walk on Rue St-Denis, I followed him. When he was in the garage, I hung out on the back porch where I could see him. When he went to Canadian Tire – he and I were both big-time browsers there – I went with him. I thought that as long as I kept him in sight I could save him. By the time school started again he seemed better, and by the end of the school year when I went to New York and left him alone, I thought he was fine.

✻

Maman knocked on the door, but she didn't open it.

"Come for breakfast, sweetheart."

"I'm not hungry."

"Please. Come."

I'd been home three days, and each morning the realization that my father was dead struck me like a slap. He couldn't die like that. He just couldn't. *Point final.* Living without my father would be like losing an arm or leg. Suddenly, I had this image of myself when I was Luc's age. I was in the garage while my father tinkered with the lawn mower. I had caught a fly and I was about to tear its legs off. Papa stopped me. The scene came back to me in a flood of pain.

I buried my face in my pillow to choke my sobs. How would I get through this day? I heard the door creak as Maman opened it. Our house is so old that it's always making noises. As long as I can remember, my bedroom door has creaked. Maman's face was pale and her hair was pulled back into a ragged ponytail.

"Honey, come and eat something. It's been so long."

"Not hungry," I replied.

"Then just have a glass of orange juice." She sat on the edge of my bed and took my hand. I turned my head to the wall.

"Why did Papa have to die? Why not Grandpa? He's always saying that he wants to go to heaven to be with Grandma."

"Life is unfair. I don't have answers for you." Maman squeezed my hand.

She went back downstairs. With a huge effort I swung my legs over the side of the bed and pulled on a T-shirt and shorts. The backpack was where I had dropped it the night I'd come home. I found the Rangers T-shirt, wadded it into a ball, and stuffed it into the bottom drawer of my dresser.

Luc was sitting in his superhero pajamas at the wobbly kitchen table. It had lost one of its legs, and Papa had replaced it with a piece of broom handle. Luc glanced up and tried to smile. When he looked back to the cereal in his bowl, he seemed not to recognize it. I wasn't hungry either. I didn't think I could keep anything down. I ran through my mental list of favorite foods to see if I could imagine being able to swallow any of them, but even the thought of double chocolate cake made me want to gag. Maman handed me two pills, and I tried to drink a glass of water.

Though Luc was sitting right there trying to sink his Cheerios with his spoon, and Maman was methodically watering the row of herbs she grew in old cans on the windowsill, and Sputnik was at the kitchen door shaking his collar, desperate to go out, the kitchen echoed with emptiness.

"Come on, Sputnik," Maman held the door open for him. "No walk for you this morning." The dog had been another great Christmas present. I'd called him Sputnik because it was easy for Luc to say. The dog's toenails clicked on the floor as he went alone into the yard.

"Will we have to move?" I'm not sure why I asked, but it seemed desperately important at the time. There would be a lot of desperate, disconnected questions from me that year.

"I don't know, Francis. Don't think about that now." Maman was washing the dishes like a robot. Her face was blank, as if someone had drained all the life out of her. When she finally stopped – I can't say she finished, she just ran down – she wiped the chipped counter with the dish cloth. She folded it carefully before she spoke again.

"We'll be beautiful today, my loves, because it's the last time we'll see your father."

"I'm staying here. I'm not going to the funeral." The very idea of burying my father seemed preposterous.

"You are coming with us, Francis. *Point final.*" She opened the kitchen door to let Sputnik back in. The dog wagged his tail and cocked his head at Maman. Her face crumpled. She sank into a chair, sobbing.

⚓

I wore an old black shirt, black pants and a black tie. The tie felt like a noose. Luc was dressed in the suit I had worn years ago when I was a ring bearer at my cousin's wedding. It was too big for him, but it was black. Maman had no black summer clothes but she'd found an old wool skirt and a black sweater with small satin bows on each shoulder. We sat down at the kitchen table to wait for Aunt Sophie.

On the kitchen wall there's a clock in the shape of Elvis Presley playing his guitar. I couldn't take my eyes off it. The hands seemed to move madly, grabbing the minutes. The more time that passed, the more I wanted to vomit. I dreaded the funeral and all the eyes that would be looking at me: "That's the kid whose father hanged himself."

Aunt Sophie arrived in a cloud of perfume, wearing a big green hat and silk scarves. She wrapped her soft, heavy arms around me. Aunt Sophie is a non-stop laugher. Her laugh is the soundtrack of her life. This morning the laugh was present, but muted, and her eyes were red and puffy. She was speaking to me, but I could not make sense of her flood of words. Finally she stopped, and we sat silently in the kitchen.

A man from the funeral home picked us up in a black limousine.

"Hello," he said in a practiced, warm voice. "My name is Jerry." I hated the limousine. It was freaking ugly and cold. I also hated every Jerry in the world. This Jerry drove slowly. I wanted him to drive fast, to skid through red lights, to smash us all into a big wall, to sail off the mountainside. That way, there would be no funeral and no eyes looking at The Suicide's Family.

~~~

It was two o'clock in the afternoon – a bright and sunny day, the kind of day you would normally enjoy because it's June, and the air is soft and scented with lilacs, and you know that school will end soon. It was not the kind of day you should spend going to your father's funeral.

Another big man met us at the door. His name was also Jerry. He smiled at us. I would have liked to pull his freaking smile off his face and stomp on it.

"Welcome, madame. I want to warn you right now: your husband is not . . ." His voice tapered off. "Death by strangulation, you know." He nodded his head and pursed his lips. "You are quite lucky to see him once again. If you had not discovered him when you did, it would have been impossible to have an open coffin. You understand, we can't leave the body exposed for very long."

The body. My father was nothing but a dead body, a piece of meat you can't keep on the counter for too long because it will turn. I wanted to punch the guy right in his big, soft, white-shirted stomach.

There were flowers everywhere, carnations mostly. Their sharp smell was nauseating. The funeral home was freezing. Everything was cold and everything was beige. I hate that color. Beige is boring. It's ugly. I hated the people who chose beige for the funeral home. The thought of them filled me with fury.

We approached the glossy oak coffin slowly, Luc, Maman, and I. Maman held our hands tightly. Hers were freezing. I didn't want to look into the coffin, but I couldn't help it.

He lay on white satin with a paler face than usual, and a turgid neck. For some reason I couldn't stop looking at his eyelashes lowered against his gray skin. Someone had curled them. I stared at him for a while, to see if his eyelids or his nostrils would move. They didn't. Luc climbed up on the prie-dieu and looked at Papa.

"Papa, I'm tired of you being dead. Get up! Play with me, please, Papa. Just for a bit. I'll help you get out of your bed. I promise I'll be a good boy."

Maman took Luc in her arms, and kissed Papa, first on the forehead, then on the lips. A chill ran through my body. I couldn't make myself touch him, not even with my fingertips.

We were alone with him for a few minutes, until the Jerrys opened the doors and people streamed in. Houston came with his father. Though Houston's been my best friend since third grade, this was the first time I'd seen him in a suit. I didn't know what to do. Should I shake his hand, hug him, kiss him?

"Francis, my sympathies." His father shook my hand.

"Thanks."

Thanks. That's all I could say. I saw my friends, Eric, Caroline, and Melanie, standing together at the back, looking uncomfortable. Melanie is the same kind of chronic laugher as Aunt Sophie, but she had a Kleenex crunched in her hand, and her eyes were red. Caroline looked pretty in her black dress. Her head was on Eric's shoulder. She's crazy about Eric; that's what she told me before we left for New York. A million years ago.

When the time came to close the coffin, one of the Jerrys took off Papa's watch and wedding ring and handed them to Maman. She gave them to me. I slipped the watch on my wrist. The ring was loose on my finger, so I put it in my pocket. The watch and ring seemed to throb as if they were charged with electricity.

～

A Jerry drove us to the cemetery. All the limo seats were the kind of white leather that hurts your eyes because it's too bright. Maman sat between Luc and me. I saw the three of us reflected in the rearview mirror. This was my new family.

～

They asked me to drop a handful of soil into the grave because I was the oldest son. I felt sweat running down my back. Afterward, Aunt Sophie took my hand, though it was all covered in dirt. Her perfume made my head ache.

Luc leaned against my leg, wanting to be picked up. I held him and he put his head on my shoulder, just like I used to with Papa when I was Luc's age. Luc knows a lot of things: he can tie his shoes, he can count to twenty, and he can sing a song in Spanish, but he's pretty much in the dark when it comes to the concept of death.

"Is there light in his coffin after they close it? Can he hear me if I talk to him?" he whispered in my ear.

I wanted him to shut up, but I didn't say anything. I buried my face in his hair.

My mother calmly dropped a handful of soil on the sleek varnished coffin, but when the cemetery guys took over and heaved dirt into the grave, she started to scream: *"WHY, MY LOVE? FOR WHAT? WHAT WILL I DO WITHOUT YOU? MY GOD, WHY DID YOU DO THIS TO ME? YOU CAN'T DO THIS TO ME! I HATE YOU! NO!"*

People craned to get a good look at The Grieving Widow. I could see Houston reaching for his father's hand. His eyes were full of pity.

You could almost taste Maman's pain in the air that we were breathing. One of her brothers wrapped his arm around her shoulders and led her stumbling to the black limousine. I helped Luc inside and slid onto the white leather seat beside him. I would have liked to hug Maman, but my arms were too weak. I wished I could dry her tears, but I was scared I might drown in them. I didn't have a shoulder for her to lean on: mine wasn't strong enough. I was only fifteen years old, skinny, weak, and scared. I sat silent and still and watched the early summer city slide by as we drove away.

❦

After the cemetery, we went to a restaurant somewhere in Old Montréal for the reception. It could have been a five-star restaurant or a chip wagon for all I cared. There was a lot of food, and Aunt Sophie was in her element, balancing a plate of pork pie, potato salad, and party sandwiches as she stood guard beside Maman. Everyone wanted to tell my mother and me that my father was too young to die, in case we hadn't realized it. Then they helped themselves to food from the buffet, and talked and laughed as if we weren't there. My godfather, Uncle Ted, sat down next to me with a beer in his hand. He isn't my favorite uncle. In fact, I don't much like any of my uncles. They're all about as warm as the St. Lawrence in January when the ice blocks the Seaway. Ted is impossible to talk to, as if he counts out the number of words he is allowed to say in a day, and if he says more than that, he'll be punished by some vengeful god.

"Well, Francis, now you are the man of the house, eh? You have to take care of your mother and your little brother. You have lots of responsibilities, you know."

Wow! Three complete sentences in a row. That's the most he's ever said to me.

"Your father was a good man," he continued. "Time will help you to forget about this."

"I guess." That's all I could think of to say. Did I inherit word-hoarding from Uncle Ted?

He patted my arm and hoisted himself to his feet. "Good luck, eh!"

Good luck. For what? Did I just buy a lottery ticket? What am I supposed to say? Thank you? Bless you? I wanted to knock over the table with its plates full of crustless party sandwiches and *tourtière* and potato salad. I hate potato salad. It's gross. I found Luc sitting by himself at a table, an untouched plate of food in front of him.

"I'm tired," he said. "I want to go home now."

"Me too." He crawled into my lap and fell asleep.

I could see my grandpa – my father's father – heading toward us. By the time he got from point A to point B with his walker, I could have played three games of Mario Bros. at the slowest speed. I didn't want to talk to him. I had had enough comfort from Uncle Ted.

"Francis. Your father is dead now."

Yes. I know. I freaking know! I thought that maybe I could pretend to faint, or pretend that I couldn't understand him. Looking back, I realize that he'd buried his son that day and could have used a big dose of comfort himself, but I had no sympathy for him. I was too shattered to comprehend anyone else's pain.

"Sorry, Grandpa. Luc has to go home to bed."

Grandpa looked at me, I think. He has a lazy eye, so I wasn't sure. That day his lazy eye enraged me.

Finally, Aunt Sophie drove us home. I put my father's wedding ring and his watch close to his picture on my desk. Luc slept with me in my bed. He curled up tight against me as if he were afraid I would vanish.

❧

I walked through the last days of school on automatic pilot.

It felt wrong to be with my friends. Houston, Caroline, Eric, Melanie. They all kept offering me reassuring smiles, but the smiles simply puzzled me. What's the point of smiling at anyone? Who wants to smile? It felt wrong to smile.

We'd been friends from the time we were kids and played on the swings at the park. We could spend all day together and then go home and spend hours on the phone. We knew all the tricks in Mario Bros.; we knew exactly what each one of us would order when we hung out at Deli Delight, home of the finest bagels you'd ever want to eat. We all knew that Houston had a crush on Caroline. He loves dancing – you should see him moon-walk, picking up static from the shag rug in the living room, all for Caroline's benefit. The problem is that Caroline didn't care about him at all as a boyfriend. She had a long-standing crush on Eric who is serious and quiet and favors black turtlenecks. Eric the Brooding Poet acts like he's oblivious. All of this had been a big deal that fascinated me. Now all the drama and intrigue and giggling scraped my nerves raw. And these were my best buddies.

I gave up going to rugby practice. My father used to love rugby.

Of course, the biggest changes were at home. After the funeral, we stopped talking about Papa. Our sorrow tunneled underground, secret and private. Luc stopped waking me up at dawn to play with him and his stupid Lego blocks.

My father's slippers waited where he had left them, side by side under the beat-up brown couch facing the TV, as if he were coming back to pull them on again. His denim jacket was still slung over the back of the rocking chair where he sat after dinner. It had muddy paw prints on it from where Sputnik had jumped up for a pat. I offered to wash it, but Maman was furious.

"That jacket is not dirty. It doesn't need to go in the washing machine," she said firmly. "It smells like him. Pine."

"But it's been there for a month."

"I said it doesn't need to be washed. *Point final.*"

~

Luc was a newborn and Maman wanted some quiet, so Papa and I walked up to the top of Mont-Royal. It's a small mountain in the middle of Montréal. It was crowded. People love the mountain during fall, especially people with dogs. They go there to breathe when they're fed up with traffic jams and stuff like that. That day, my dad taught me how to recognize *petit thé des bois*. It's a kind of grass you can eat when you're hungry and lost. I ran ahead and when I retraced my steps, looking for him, he jumped out from behind a tree, yelling *Boo!* I hated it when he did that, but he loved to surprise me.

Right after Papa died I went back up to the top of Mont-Royal and sat under the same tree, waiting for him to jump out and yell *Boo!* I sat under that tree until it grew dark, but nothing happened, maybe because I was fifteen and when you're fifteen you're too old for scary games.

~

It's funny, the things you miss. In those first few weeks I fretted, because Papa had promised to show me a trick for holding my poker hand and he was going to give me a tip on bluffing. He took all his secrets with him.

<center>~~~</center>

Montréal features January Sundays so cold that the only thing you want to do is stay home with a bowl of soup and a piece of warm apple pie. The Seaway was frozen over and Papa was on shore leave with time on his hands. After lunch he made an announcement. "You are seven years old, son," he said solemnly. "The time has come for you to learn how to play poker."

Maman was at the sink washing the dishes with lime dish detergent. I have always loved that smell – I don't know what it reminds me of, but who cares. Whenever I smell limes I think of the time before Luc was born when the house was snug and the roof was sound and outside the frosty windows the garage and the garden were neat and well-kept.

Papa cleared off the chipped table and made a pile of pennies in the middle. He cracked open a fresh deck of cards.

"Ben, why are you using new cards with the boy? Those are for company." Maman didn't sound angry, but it was true. During weekdays, when my father was at home and my parents played cards, they used an old grimy deck. For special guests, they brought out slippery fresh cards.

"Because today I'm teaching the boy to play poker. Fish is for babies. It's time to show him how men play."

I was thrilled. I thought that once we played a hand, I would get up from the table a foot taller and I'd know all my multiplication tables by heart. It didn't happen, of course. In fact, I've never learned the multiplication tables – that's why I rank the calculator at the top of the list of the world's greatest inventions. I watched Papa make the cards waterfall through his hands in an orderly ribbon. I wanted to be able to make them obey like he did, but my fingers were too short and awkward.

Sometimes Maman played with us, but she wasn't very good at it: she wasn't observant enough. When people play poker, it's important to observe them, especially their eyes, when they are dealt their new cards. Papa said that learning how to play poker is like getting an education in a human being. You have to learn about his strengths, his weaknesses, his nervous tics, and his moods. I guess I didn't play enough poker with my father to realize that he had hidden cards up his sleeves. I didn't know that he could cheat.

At first, we only played for pennies. But after a few weeks, when I learned how to hold my cards close enough so that no one could see them, Papa taught me how to play "real" cards like straight poker and blackjack. He let me use the pennies in my little china piggybank. He often won, but even when I lost, my penny pig never grew lighter. Papa always replaced my coins. One day when I was twelve, I couldn't find my pig. It wasn't on my shelf or my desk. When I asked my mother where it was, she said: "It's been magically changed into groceries." She didn't laugh.

I never asked about my little pig again. She didn't have to tell me that Papa had no work. Life had begun to change.

3 | INJUSTICE

The long, hot summer finally ended. Luc wore new shoes to kindergarten, and we took his picture standing proudly at the front door. I didn't want to take the shine off his day, but I dreaded going back to school. All I wanted to do was hole up in my bedroom and play guitar. I needed to be lonely.

The first shock of the day was that Mr. Enrique had left the school. We didn't know why, but apparently, his blind cat, Rococo, had died. We got a new Spanish teacher.

When the First-Day-of-Class commotion was over, Mr. Lunes rapped on his desk.

"What is a preposition?"

I had no idea and hoped that he wasn't calling on me. He was.

"Young man. What is your name?"

« *Me llamo Francis Gregory.* »

« *¡Muy bien! ¿Y qué es el nombre de tu padre?* »

I could feel everybody looking at me. There was an embarrassed shuffling of feet.

« *Mi padre se llama Ben.* »

« *¡Muy bien! ¿Qué hace tu padre en la vida?* »

What did my father do? The class sat in frozen fascination as if they were watching a trainwreck.

« *Por favor, ¿qué hace tu padre en la vida?* »

I wanted to grab Mr. Lunes by the throat and break his neck, but I didn't. When I was little and I didn't like a Christmas gift, I would throw it at the wall. I'd learned not to do that anymore, because when you're fifteen you're kind of a part of adult society, and you have mastered the art of pretending to love nauseating Chia Pets or gray woollen socks or a book on saints. That lesson stood me in good stead for staying in my seat and answering Mr. Lunes' questions. As opposed to committing murder.

« *Mi padre es marinero.* »

« *¡Muy bien!* »

I had said, "My father *is* a sailor," instead of "*was*." I couldn't say my father was dead even though the whole class knew the truth, and Houston and Caroline and Eric and Melanie had all been to my father's funeral. They would have had to have some sort of group amnesia to have missed the big news that my father had committed suicide. I was Son of Suicide Man. I could picture the cartoon on TV: *Suicide Man Against the Terrible Smiley Face. Suicide Man and the Magic Rope in the Attic.* Ugly thoughts. Unbelievably, nobody ever mentioned that Spanish class to me. I was grateful.

At our school people sniff out differences like killer sharks going for blood. You're supposed to be free to express yourself, but you'd better be the same as everybody else – or else. You'd think I was used to being different because we were poorer than my friends. I'd never been one of those kids who could afford expensive clothes, and have the latest gizmos as soon as they came out. We didn't have a second home in Florida or a cottage in the Laurentians. We didn't have a boat or a second car in the driveway. Nothing like that. We didn't even have a computer. Still, being poor was not as big a deal as being Son of Suicide Man. Now, that was something different. Looking back, maybe the other kids teased me or talked about me behind my back, but to tell you the truth, if they did, I didn't notice. Grief is an anesthetic, but I don't recommend it.

✴

One night as I lay in bed staring at the barren stretch of ceiling, a new thought started to gnaw at me. What if my mother died too? What would happen to me and Luc? I left my door open to listen for any creaks on the stairs, in case my mother was headed for the attic.

One day Maman was fifteen minutes late coming home from the post office where she worked. She tried to get as much overtime as she could, but she always called me to let me know. This time she didn't.

My whole body shook as I pressed the buttons on the phone. "Hi! Is Lisa Gregory still there?"

"No, sorry. She left, maybe ten minutes ago."

"Are you sure she's not there?"

"Yes, I am. Sorry about that. Is it urgent?"

"No, no. It's Francis, her son."

"Oh! Hi, Francis! How are you?"

"Fine."

Fine was apparently the right word to say, even though I felt anything but fine. I turned on both the radio and the TV, in case there was news of an accident. Now that my father was dead, any calamity was possible. I thought that if Maman had died, I would die too. All I had in the world was her and my little Luc. The thought of losing either of them was unbearable.

I finally saw her car turn into the driveway. I can't describe the relief. She threw her bag and her keys on the hall table, like a baseball player throwing a ball with all of his strength. She sat down on the bottom stair to take off her winter boots. There had been an early snowfall.

I wanted to yell: *Do you have any idea how worried I've been!* Instead, I said, "Maman, I made vegetable soup for you and Luc."

"That's nice, but I'm not hungry, honey." She sounded exhausted.

"You have to eat something, Maman."

"I will, dear, later."

It was always the same thing. Later. She didn't eat anymore. Each night, she would stand at the kitchen counter peeling onions – maybe to be able to cry in front of us without having to hide her tears. Her frantic cleaning of the summer was over. After she put the food on the table and fed Sputnik, she would go into the living room and sit watching the fire in the fireplace until she fell asleep on the couch, Papa's wool vest clutched in her arms.

I cleaned up the kitchen quietly and put Luc to bed. In those days I was trying my best to be good. I wanted to show everyone how strong I was, even if deep down I wanted to collapse and disappear under the ugly living room rug forever.

⚬⚬⚬

Snow muffled the trees and roofs like a white shroud. I had started getting stuck on words, wanting to say them or write them over and over. You won't be surprised to learn that *shroud* was one of those words. This time it fit.

Luc brought home a form letter from kindergarten advising us that he would be a lamb in the Christmas pageant. The teacher had added a hand-written note that we were not to worry. There was a leftover lamb costume from last year's Easter pageant.

"When are we getting the Christmas tree?" he asked at supper.

"I don't know," said Maman. She looked at me with a slight shake of her head. The Christmas decorations were neatly packed in a box we kept in the attic. No one had been up to the attic since Papa died there. "I just don't know."

❀

Though we didn't talk about my father he was everywhere in the house. Each room was rich with memories: the kitchen table that could instantly be transformed into a card table, that hideous living room carpet that turned into a perfect wrestling mat, the brown sofa cushions that morphed into the most comfortable tent in the whole world.

❀

"Francis, there's a call for you." Maman shouted up from the living room without moving from the couch.

"Who is it?"

"Houston."

"Tell him I'm busy." Five minutes later Maman knocked on my door. I was staring at a page in a Superman comic instead of studying math. Let me take this opportunity to mention once again how very much I hate math. It is supposed to be logical, but nothing in life is logical. I also hate math class because Houston sits right in front of me and he spends every possible second clowning around for Caroline's benefit. All that stupid childish stuff was getting on my nerves.

Maman opened my door carefully, as if she was afraid it might be booby-trapped.

"Are you mad at Houston? He's called five times in the last two days, and you always say that you are busy."

"I don't want to talk about it."

"Houston was your best friend. Now you won't talk to him or anyone else. What happened?"

"Nothing."

"Did you have an argument? Did he say something?"

"There's nothing wrong! Leave me alone."

She shut the door quickly. From behind it, she said:

"Well . . . I don't know what to say. . . . If you want to talk to me, you know that you can, sweetheart, Maman is here. I love you, honey."

Of course I knew that I could talk to her, but I didn't want to. I didn't want to cry in front of her. I thought that if I cried, she would too and we'd never stop. The plain truth was that I didn't want to talk to Houston because he loved a good laugh, and because he still had his father.

I was walking around with this big ugly thing inside my chest that actually hurt. Whoever came up with the image of being brokenhearted really knew what he was talking about. A nice twist of the knife is, that just when you need to distract yourself with books or with music or with movies or with your friends, you can't. The pain fills up every nook and cranny of your mind, and you can't focus on the things you used to enjoy. You end up feeling completely alone.

I wasn't about to dump any of this sick stuff on Luc. He was just a baby. As long as he had *Sesame Street* and Sputnik and Aunt Sophie he seemed to be fine, but who knows? My friends didn't get it either. Here's what my friends knew about pain: not much. Caroline's idea of pain was having a crush on a person who was obviously much more interested in being a moody poet in a black turtleneck and who listened to Bob Dylan than he was in her. Houston's emotional state rose and fell with the fortunes of the Montréal Expos. As for Eric, who was a short redhead with a pug nose and braces, in his heart he was a Mississippi blues man who carried the woes of the world on his shoulders. But he had no idea about loss. Even the dog he got when he was a little kid was still alive. As for Melanie, it's hard to know what went on in the mind of Serial Giggler. She could laugh for Canada. Don't get me wrong. I'm not some kind of monster who wanted my friends to suffer. I knew in my head that I used to have a riot with them, but it was like someone drained all the color out of being in their company.

You'd think that in the Larger Fish Tank of School, there'd be other kids in my boat, but I didn't know any. There was a girl, Sydney, in my biology class, whose

parents got a divorce that was so ugly it made the news-
papers. There were other kids whose parents had divorced
in a less dramatic way, but I didn't know anyone whose
father or mother had died. I was ashamed to say that my
father was dead. I was ashamed to say he committed
suicide. I didn't want to be seen as an extraterrestrial of
some kind.

⚬⚬⚬

Here's some advice: steer clear of canned Christmas cheer
if you're feeling down. It will kill you. Right after school
on the first Friday of December, I went to the mall. It was
lousy with Christmas cheer. Over the loud speaker Bing
Crosby sang "White Christmas" three times in a row. I was
walking down the electronics aisle at Canadian Tire when
I thought I saw my father. He wore a coat like Papa's, and
combed his hair the same way. I followed him, but he kept
disappearing between the rows of blenders and tool kits.
Finally, I turned into an aisle and there he was, reaching for
a toaster. I could see his face. It wasn't Papa.

⚬⚬⚬

After Luc was in bed and Maman was asleep in front of
the fireplace, I snapped on Sputnik's leash. It was a bril-
liantly clear, cold night. As I walked down the dark street,
I could see in the windows where blinds hadn't been drawn
for the night. The people inside seemed impossibly happy
and warm. I walked down to Houston's house, which is

not far from mine. I thought that maybe we could talk or play Nintendo, like we used to in the days when we both believed that the Transformers would save the world, but when I got near his house I could see that he and his dad were in the garage fiddling with the car. I turned back before he noticed me.

~~~

You might be wondering where the rest of our family was all those weeks. Nowhere, is where, except for Aunt Sophie. Every week or so, Maman took us to visit Grandpa in the nursing home. He'd ask where Papa was. Sometimes he'd call me Ben. Maybe nature was being kind to him by letting him forget that his son was dead.

As for all my uncles – and there are tons of them – I don't remember seeing them that year. Our family is big, but that's not unusual in Québec. My mother has six brothers, and my father, ten. And then there are all my aunts and their husbands. They phoned Maman every now and then, but I don't remember any of them turning up to see me or Luc. My father had been a disgrace, a suicide.

Uncle Ted did a vanishing act. For the first time in my life I needed him. I wanted him to call me to say something like: "Hey Francis! What are you doing this afternoon? I have two tickets to see the Expos. Wanna come with me?"

Or, "Wanna help me to fix the old clunker? The muffler is broken, my boy. And you know what? After that, I could even teach you how to drive."

He never did. I heard Maman tell Aunt Sophie that Uncle Ted liked to drink water, the kind that you put in a tray and it becomes ice cubes, and then it swims in a glass of Scotch.

~~~

I wanted to make sure that Christmas was okay for Luc's sake. To avoid going up to the attic for the Christmas boxes, I had bought new tinsel and Christmas decorations at Canadian Tire. Luc was curled up in front of the TV watching *Barney* when I came in with my packages. The curtains were drawn against the dark, even though it was only five in the afternoon. I went into the kitchen and put the bags on the table.

"Why did you buy that stuff, Francis? How much did it all cost?" Maman sounded exhausted.

"It's Christmas, in case you haven't noticed!"

"What did you use for money?"

"Last year's birthday money from Grandpa."

She looked at me as if I was Spock from *Star Trek*. Spock used to scare me. Actually, so did Barbra Streisand. When I was little, I would lie in my bed in the dark, afraid that they would come into my room and kidnap me. I was a weird kid, what can I say? It was a terrifying thought at the time, but now it would have been a relief to have them come for me.

Frowning, Maman poured herself a cup of black coffee.

"Next time, before you buy junk, think of buying food instead. It would be more useful."

That was all the thanks I got. I left the Christmas decorations in their plastic bags piled on the kitchen table, and went to my bedroom.

Despite the decorations and Luc's stage début in a pink and white lamb costume, Christmas was a big zero. Now I could add Christmas holidays to the long list of things I had grown to hate, which included going to church on Sunday and locking my keys in the house. Aunt Sophie suggested that we go to a restaurant for Christmas dinner, and Grandpa invited us to the Family Fun Christmas at the nursing home. Maman told them we needed the time alone, so Luc and I sat in the living room, with tinsel tacked around the windows and across the mantel, and a crackling fire in the fireplace. That was our big Christmas entertainment, watching the fire.

Since I can remember, we've had a family routine. At six o'clock on the nose before we sat down to a dinner of salmon, Maman and Papa handed out the Christmas gifts. Luc and I had bought Maman a candle that smelled of pine in a holder shaped like a Scottie dog. She wiped her eyes when she opened the box and thanked us.

"I'm sorry I didn't wrap your presents, boys, but here they are. Francis, this is for you."

It was a knapsack for school. I'd been hoping for a PlayStation, but I knew I wasn't going to get it.

"And Luc, here's something for you too." A Fraggle Rock lunch box. Maman didn't wait for us to say anything. White-faced, she ran upstairs to her bedroom. I could hear her close her door. She slept all night.

～～～

I was left alone with Luc. It was too early to put him to bed so we sat on the rug, Sputnik between us, watching *It's a Wonderful Life* on TV. I prayed for the Apocalypse or the Third World War or the Return of the Extra-terrestrial or Barbra Streisand – anything that would get me out of this empty, sad house.

When I went back to school after what could only charitably be called the holidays, Houston was full of news about all his gifts – a PlayStation, a new computer, a snowboard, Vuarnet sunglasses – his father had given him. I had nothing to say.

～～～

Although months had passed since Papa's suicide, Luc was convinced that Papa would come back. I was sitting on the bathroom floor thumbing through a comic book while Luc played in the tub. He ducked under the surface to rinse his hair and bobbed up, rubbing his eyes.

"When will Papa come home, Francis? Maman says he's gone for eternity. What's eternity?"

Luc was always ambushing us with questions that stumped us.

"Can Papa stop being dead for my birthday? Did I kill Papa because I told him that I didn't love him anymore? I didn't mean it, Francis."

I was trying my best, but all I wanted was for him to shut up. *Did I kill Papa because I left him alone to go to New York?*

Saturday night, late. I heard the TV blaring, but when I went downstairs the living room was empty. I felt a cold blast and realized that the front door was wide open. I went out on the porch. Luc was standing on the walk in his bare feet.

"Luc!"

He didn't seem to hear me.

"What are you doing, Luc?"

I saw that he had taken the clothesline from the back-yard, and had wrapped it around Sputnik's neck.

"For God's sake, what are you freaking doing?"

"I want Sputnik to commit suicide."

"Stop it! Are you freaking crazy?"

I leaped down the stairs and ripped the clothesline from around the dog's neck.

"I want Sputnik to find Papa."

I didn't know what to do or what to say. I felt so lost. Sputnik shook himself and plodded up the stairs. He stopped on the porch and looked back at us reproachfully before going into the house.

Luc went into High Question Mode. "Does it hurt to die? What do we eat under the ground? Who will tell Papa when to come back?"

I squatted close to him, in the snow. What else could I do but listen?

"Francis, Luc, what are you doing there? Are you two crazy? You'll catch cold. Come back in the house this instant!" Maman sounded frightened.

I've never been so cold. The sky was full of stars. I wanted Luc to understand once and for all that Papa would never come back, and that he had to leave Sputnik alone – poor dog. Luc's big blue eyes looked at me as if I were Superman.

"Luc, when we die, we don't need to eat anymore."

"What about chocolate?"

"Not even chocolate."

"Will I die, too?"

"Not today for sure, Luc. Not tomorrow either. Don't worry about it."

"Can I talk to Papa while he's dead?"

I wished he could. I wished I could, too. "Of course you can. In your heart. You can tell him all the things you want to in your heart."

"Can I talk to him with you sometime?"

"We can do it right now if you want."

My eyes were starting to water, but I didn't want to cry in front of Luc. I took a deep breath, and carried him up to his bedroom. I could hear Maman below us. In the kitchen, the tap was running. Luc pulled on his socks and I handed him his teddy bear.

We knelt at the foot of his bed, and I showed him how to fold his hands and pray, something my family didn't do a lot, except for funerals, baptisms, and weddings. To tell the truth, I had no idea what I was doing, but Luc was looking at me with such trust that I knew I had to wing it.

"Okay, this is what you do, Luc. You have to repeat after me."

"After me," he said, squeezing his eyes tight shut.

"Papa."

"Papa," he said.

"Good night from the bottom of my heart."

"Good night from the heart of my bottom."

"Stop it. That's not funny." I tried to sound stern.

"Sorry. Good night from the bottom of my heart."

"Papa, I love you so much." I whispered the words.

"Me too," he said.

I kissed him on the cheek and gave him a bear hug. He climbed into his bed. I straightened his covers around him and smoothed his hair.

There was a photo that I took last May in a Snoopy frame on the little table beside Luc's bed. The crabapple tree in the backyard was in full blossom. Maman stood in front of it, next to Papa. Luc was perched on Papa's shoulders, laughing right into the camera. The blossoms surrounded them in a pink halo. I looked at the photo, turned off the light, closed the door, went to my bedroom, and cried.

4 | SADNESS

1993. Bill Clinton succeeded George Bush as president – no more vomiting on the Japanese prime minister. In New York City, a van bomb parked below the North Tower of the World Trade Center went off, killing six people and injuring over a thousand. Kim Campbell became Canada's first female prime minister. For about five minutes. Yasser Arafat and Yitzhak Rabin shook hands in Washington, DC after signing a peace accord. *Jurassic Park*, and *Schindler's List* were released, and k.d. lang with Eric Clapton won a Grammy for the best pop vocal performance. I started to notice these things, but there was still a hard slog ahead of me.

~~~

As the winter dragged on I began to spend Friday afternoons riding my bike to the Mount Royal Cemetery instead of going to school. It's a good twenty-minute ride, all up hill, which I'm here to tell you is long enough to freeze off your ears and your nose twice over. I didn't want anyone to know, especially Maman. I knew she went to the cemetery too, because there were often footprints in the snow and fresh flowers on the grave, but I didn't want her to find out what I was doing. She would have flipped about my cutting classes, for one thing. But mostly it felt like something so personal and so private that I had to keep it to myself. I would take a book to read and sit by the tombstone until I was too cold to stand it. Sometimes I had whole conversations with him:

"Hey, Papa! How's life up there? Do you know how much I miss you? Luc talks about you all the time. He thinks you will come back. I've tried to explain, but he doesn't get it. Sputnik doesn't get much exercise these days. Are you mad that mostly we just let him out in the backyard? For Maman, it's different. She barely talks anymore. She goes to work, comes home, peels onions, cooks dinner, washes the dishes, and sits in front of the fire. That's about it for her. We haven't touched your slippers or your jacket since you've been gone. It's strange to say *gone*. If only I knew where you've gone, but I don't."

Sometimes I felt close to him. Other times I felt like he was a galaxy away.

It was the last gray day of a damp and frigid March. Aunt Sophie had picked up Luc for an excursion to the doughnut shop, and Maman was still at work. We have a candle shaped like an owl that sits on the mantelpiece in the living room. I got it down, set it in the middle of the kitchen table, and lit it. I pulled out one of the kitchen chairs and placed it in the center of the room.

"Papa, if you can hear me, please, make the chair move."

It didn't.

My mother spent more and more time at work. She said she did overtime to pay the taxes on the house. She developed a mantra: "I pray to God for good health so that I can keep my job. That's all I ask." The more she said it, the more terrified I was that she'd get sick and die.

I skipped more and more school, partly because I could barely stand to be with Houston. When I couldn't weasel away from him, he'd rattle on about being in love with a girl from the twelfth grade. Love. What an improbable idea. Though it was a refreshing change from the Song of Caroline, it made me crazy to listen to him. One spring day when everything had turned to mud, but there was that softness in the air that can transform Montréal into the most beautiful place on earth, I was unlocking my bike at the stand in front of the school. I had just enough

time to ride up to the cemetery and back before it was
time to get Luc from day care. I looked up to see Houston
standing in front of me.

"Francis, dude, what's going on?"

"Nothing. What do you mean?"

"Stop it. I'm not as stupid as I look."

"I never said you were stupid."

"You're never home when I call, and you don't stop by
my place when you take a walk after supper like you used
to. You know what?"

"What?"

"Maybe you lost your father. Okay. I'm sorry for you.
But I lost my friend. I lost you." His face was splotchy red.

"I miss you too, dude," I said.

"It's hard for me to say this, but I want my buddy back.
The guy with the weird hair and the skateboard under
his arm. You know, that spoiled little brat? Wait a second.
That's not you! That's Bart Simpson."

"Easy mistake." I straddled my bike, not knowing what
else to say.

Houston continued, his voice rising. "But seriously,
you're my best friend. Remember when you came to my
place every night for two whole months in grade five
because I wrecked my neck break dancing? Where's that
guy, Francis? Where is he? I'm looking for him, you
know, but he's turned into some sort of grief freak. I miss
him, you know, dude?"

Houston was crying. I had never seen him cry before – except when he wrecked his neck.

"I don't know where you went, but come back." He hugged me, right there in front of the bike rack. I started crying, too. If anyone was watching us, and I'm sure they were, I didn't notice.

"I'm sorry, man," I said.

"No, I'm the one who's sorry."

"I feel like I'm in a girlie movie."

"Me too."

We laughed.

"Want to come to my place tonight? You have to try my new PlayStation. You'll see, it's freaking great!"

"I don't know."

"Come on, Francis!"

I realized how much I had missed him, and I nodded.

"Great! What about seven-thirty?"

I hadn't forgotten about the cemetery, exactly, but pushing my bike, I walked home with Houston. When we got to my place, he put a hand on my shoulder, like he used to. Neither one of us said a word, but we were friends again.

Beginning of April. The days were growing longer and the boulders of frozen, dirty snow that had choked our street were almost gone.

I had skipped school that day – and the two days before – to go to the cemetery. Crocuses and tulips were sprouting on the lawn.

When I got home Luc was sitting cross-legged in front of the TV, watching *Sesame Street*. My mother was rooted to her usual spot in front of the kitchen sink, washing dishes as if she hadn't moved since morning.

"How is it going, sweetheart?"

"Good. How was your day?" I rummaged in the cupboard for a cookie. I snapped it in two and gave half to Sputnik.

"Good. Yours?"

"Good, I just told you."

"What classes did you have today?"

"Uh . . . math and biology." There was something about her voice that should have warned me.

"What did you learn today?"

"Lots of things. Why?"

"Because the school secretary called to tell me that you didn't show up."

She dried her hands on the dishcloth and looked at me with an I-know-everything-so-don't-try-to-lie-to-me expression that would freeze a rhino in its tracks. "Where were you, Francis?"

I don't know if I was ashamed or afraid or angry or embarrassed. I just knew I didn't want to tell her.

"Where were you? Don't make me ask you again!"

"I was at the cemetery. Happy now?"

"What were you doing there?"

I stared at the gray swirls in the linoleum tiles on the floor. "I was visiting Papa."

She didn't say anything for a couple of seconds. She just looked at me with a fed up expression as if I were six years old eating ice cream and getting more on the floor than into my mouth. *Sorry I'm a mess, Maman.*

"Next Monday, instead of going to the cemetery, you're going to the psychologist at school. I made an appointment for you."

"I don't need a psychologist. I'm not a freak."

"You'll go anyway! *Point final.*"

I stormed up to my room and banged the door behind me. I grabbed my guitar and sat on my bed hammering at the strings, but I couldn't block out the sound of Luc crying in the living room. He was probably scared that what was left of his family was cracking some more.

5 | PLAYING GAMES

The next morning, I slept in. When I came down to breakfast the house was empty. Sputnik's leash was missing from its hook so I knew that Maman and Luc had taken him for a walk. There was a small wooden chest on the table. I read the note folded on top of it:

Francis, this was Papa's. Take care of it.

I held it for a moment before I opened its metal clasp. Inside was a battered pipe I'd never seen Papa smoke, a couple of old snapshots of him as a young man standing on the pier, and a deck of playing cards that was at least as old as the pictures. When I shook the cards out of their box, a folded piece of paper fell to the floor. I smoothed it out:

August 14, 1953. We, the Loyal Order of the Companions of Poker, pledge to meet on August 14, 1993 at 9 p.m. for a rematch at The Sailor, 142 Chester Street, Toronto. Password: Black Jack.

In 1953, my father would have been just twenty years old, but his handwriting hadn't changed. I'd never heard him talk about the Loyal Order of the Companions of Poker or any reunion. In fact, the only time I remember him talking about Toronto was when he was on a rant about the Maple Leafs. I refolded the paper and put it back between the cards. I carried the box upstairs and stowed it with the Rangers jersey in my bottom drawer. Despite these little glitches: the note in the box was obviously written in fun, it was almost forty years old, and it referred to something that everybody involved had probably forgotten – *if* they were still alive, I felt like I had won the lottery. I know it sounds crazy, but I thought that if I could just get to the reunion, I'd meet up with my father. I can't explain it. It's not like I was delusional. I knew what was real and what wasn't. I just didn't want to accept it, that's all.

6 | INVENTION

When I came home from school one rainy spring afternoon, the back door was unlocked, so I knew Maman was home from work. She was sitting on the living room floor with photographs scattered around her.

"I miss him so much." She hugged herself and rocked as she sobbed. "I had an urge to look at our wedding pictures. We were so happy in them." Finally she wiped her eyes with the shreds of Kleenex in her hand. "I'm sorry. I didn't realize how late it is. It's time to make dinner."

I longed to talk about Papa with her, but it was as if all my feelings were locked in a safe and the key had gotten lost. I went upstairs to my bedroom without saying anything.

When spring comes to our street and the snow recedes, the crop of mittens and hats that have been frozen in drifts all winter begin to surface like exotic flowers. I started to notice that there were whole hours when the grief ebbed and left patches of normal life behind it. It was like finding a lost mitten when you've almost forgotten about it. That's when I would think about what we'd be having for supper or what was playing at the movies or whether I should do my Spanish homework before my science assignment. Slowly, slowly I began to prefer being with my friends to being alone. Their jokes were still pretty lame, but I knew they were trying their best for me, and that counted for a lot.

The nights remained gruesome long after the days became easier. Hard as it was to accept that my father was dead, it was a piece of cake compared to accepting that he'd committed suicide. Night after long night I would lie in my bed thinking of him hanging from a crossbeam in the attic, surrounded by boxes of our baby clothes and an old sewing machine and gold Christmas balls. It would be easier to believe that he was killed by a stranger than to admit he'd killed himself, because then there would be somebody for me to hate. I couldn't hate my father.

A man from the insurance company came to talk to Maman.

"Finish giving Luc his lunch," she called from the front door. I cut Luc's toast into soldiers, poured tomato soup into his Kermit bowl, and put on coffee for Maman and the insurance guy.

When I carried two mugs into the dining room for them, they were sitting across from each other with papers spread all over the table. The agent's briefcase lay open between them. I could see pens and a calculator and a calendar neatly arranged in it. Neither of them looked at me.

Without warning Maman stood up, stuffed the papers into the briefcase and threw the whole thing at the man with impressive force. He ducked, and the case crashed to the floor.

Maman stomped out of the room and up the stairs. I could hear her ranting as she paced up and down the hall above us.

The agent straightened his jacket and picked up the briefcase.

"You won't be able to collect on your father's life insurance," he explained, red-faced. "I'm afraid it was not a *natural* death."

I snapped the leash on Sputnik and dug Luc's jacket out of the closet. "Come on, kiddo. We're going to the park."

"Why?"

"I think Maman might want to be alone." I could hear a variety of furious slammings and stompings above us.

It was a bright April day. Luc climbed up on the swing, and I pushed him. I didn't know how much he'd taken in of the scene Maman had created, but just in case, I wanted him to forget about it. I wanted him to soar high in the sky. In French we say as high as a grown-up's hat. He shrieked with laughter.

We walked Sputnik to the off-leash part of the park and found an empty bench. Sputnik did a play bow to a passing collie that looked like it was carrying a tree in its mouth. The two of them took off, playing tug-the-branch.

"You know what, Francis?" Luc sounded as if he had worked out a puzzle. "Papa is dead."

"Yes, that's true."

"And that's why Maman cries a lot."

"Yes, I know."

He trained his blue, trusting eyes on me. I hated when he looked at me like that. "Francis, teach me how to play the guitar."

"Why?"

"Because I don't want you to be alone." I didn't have to wonder whether or not Luc had figured out the insurance stuff. Nothing much got by him.

My little brother. My little Luc. It hit me how much life is like poker. Some people draw all the good cards, and others only dream that they'll get a decent hand some day. Luc's cards were pretty dire for a kid so young.

If I were God, if He exists, I would make a rule that people get to send the person they've lost three messages. They could ask for advice or tell them that they were loved and are missed. One of the questions I would ask Papa is, how do I take care of Luc? I don't know what the other questions would be.

When we got home from the park and I had put a plate of cookies in front of Luc and wiped the mud off Sputnik's paws and hairy belly, I found Maman in her usual place, curled up at the end of the brown corduroy couch, Papa's vest clutched tight against her body. Despite the sheer nuttiness of her having built a fire on this warm day, she seemed much calmer. A TV evangelist was pacing back and forth on the screen. She was watching him punch the air with the sound off.

"Maman?"

"Yes, honey?"

"Do you believe in God?" It had never occurred to me to wonder what she believed, but now it seemed urgent for me to know.

"Yes, I do."

"Why?"

"Because it makes me feel better."

"That's it?"

She turned her attention to me. "I want to think that your father is in some kind of paradise and that he's looking out for us," she said firmly.

"You really believe that?"

"Yes. I like to think that he is our guardian angel. You want to know something, honey? Sometimes, especially when I'm here, in front of the fireplace, I feel some kind of a presence around me. I don't know. Maybe it's him."

I wanted to believe her, but I wasn't sure what to think. I never felt any presence, ever. She reached out to ruffle my hair and smiled, really smiled at me for the first time since last June.

7 | HOUSTON

That old Grief Monster had its own schedule. Just when I thought my head was clear of the water, it would rise up like a sea serpent and drag me down again. I could be pointing to the pizza in the cafeteria line, or trying to work out an equation in math when it would grab me by the legs and pull me under, so that I felt like water was pouring into my lungs. I thought I had cried all the tears that a human being could possibly cry, but evidently there is no limit. I *was* turning into some sort of grief freak. I discovered every single spot in the school where you can cry without being seen. You'd be amazed at how many there are.

Everybody liked Houston. I'm not saying that just because he was my best friend. It was impossible not to like the goofiest guy in the entire universe. He made people think that the world was one good laugh. When Aunt Sophie first met him, she shook her head fondly. "That boy is a tonic. That's what he is, a tonic."

It just goes to show what shape I was in when I tell you that Houston, my friend since forever, and the sweetest guy you can imagine, was driving me crazy. Since the day at the bike rack I'd been spending more time with him, but it wasn't easy. I never realized until Papa died that he talked nonstop about his father. Life at their house sounded like a neverending season of *Father Knows Best*. There was the "Houston Get's His Dad's Old Electric Razor" episode, and the "Houston and His Dad Go to the Mall and Can't Find Their Car," episode. He treated me to "Houston's Dad Teaches Him to Drive." He had hit sixteen.

"My father wants me to learn on his car because he says it has all these safety features. It's a real drag because he has an old man's car. Plus it's white."

"You're pretty lucky," I said.

"Are you serious? I'm going to be driving a car that's white. White!"

"At least you've got someone to teach you."

"How about one of your uncles?"

"Not a chance. They all have their own kids. They don't need anybody else's."

Houston had hit yet another sore spot. I was full of them at the time. I know it sounds horrible now, but I sincerely wished that Houston's father would drop dead.

~~~

There was this amazing girl in my French class. She was from Barrie, somewhere in Ontario – you know, the *center* of Canada. Her name was Julia and she always smelled like lily of the valley. She'd been there since September, but I only actually noticed her in the spring.

Houston saw me doodling her name on my three-ring binder. He passed me a note.

"Forget it. She only likes guys who shave."

On the way home from school I stopped at the drugstore and bought a package of plastic razors. I locked myself in the bathroom and sat on the edge of the tub to read the instructions on how not to slit my throat in French and then in English. I looked at myself in the mirror, and thought: *Papa, I could sure use some advice right about now.*

Luc pounded on the door and I jumped.

"Let me in, Francis! I have to pee."

"Hold on, Luc." I'd cut myself in five places. I stuck bits of toilet paper on my face, like I remembered Papa doing. I didn't want to think about what I'd look like tomorrow morning in French class. Julia liked guys who shave. I didn't know where she stood on guys who looked like a double pepperoni pizza.

I needed Papa's advice badly, not only about cars and shaving and stuff, but also about girls. I had been friends with Caroline and Melanie for years, but the pathetic fact was that I knew absolutely nothing about girls except that they smell good and giggle a lot. I had never kissed a girl.

~~~

I finally emerged from the bathroom and a desperate Luc pushed by me. Maman was at the linen closet in the hall, putting away freshly ironed sheets.

"My poor baby, what did you do to yourself?" She took my chin in her hand.

"I don't want to talk about it."

"Oh! I see. You tried to shave!" She looked at me fondly.

She had said *tried*.

"No. I thought I'd dab your red lipstick all over my face to see if you would notice." I could tell that she was trying hard not to smile.

"Next time, ask me and I'll help." She gave me a quick kiss and turned back to her nice, orderly laundry. I was furious.

8 | HELP

It was Friday. The highlight of my day would be my appointment with the school psychologist. I'd rather have stuck pins in my head. It was Maman's idea. I was supposed to see him twice a week, right after math class. His office was beside the library and across the hall from the boys' washroom on the second floor. I was terrified that somebody would see me coming out of his office. The Suicide's Son times the Shrink equals Weirdness squared.

Anyway, that's what I used to think, and for the first couple of weeks I held on to the idea like a dog with a bone. To be honest, I was so uncomfortable being there that I don't remember much of what happened the first hour. Mr. Bergeron was fortyish, balding, and wore big thick smeared glasses on his round face. There were photos of his sons on his desk – I guessed that's who they were – and a Rubik's Cube. I was about to learn the man owned, and played with, a Rubik's Cube. Nerd alert. I wrote *Rubik's Cube* four times in my notebook. It proved to be an excellent time filler. Try it.

Meanwhile, Mr. Bergeron was also busy scribbling on his yellow note pad, but I doubt that he was writing *Rubik's Cube*. His silence was getting on my nerves.

"Do you play any sports?" I thought I'd get the ol' conversation ball rolling.

"Yes. Sometimes I play tennis with my two sons." I'd guessed right. I thought that his sons were lucky – not to have a father like Mr. Bergeron, but simply to have a father.

"How old are they?" I looked at the photo on his desk.

"Fifteen and seventeen."

"Are you teaching them to drive?"

"We don't have a car."

I'm supposed to get help from a grown man who doesn't own a car? "But if you had one, would you?"

He put his grease-smudged glasses on his desk. "I don't think so. They're too young."

"But will you teach them someday?"

"Maybe."

A long silence ensued. I don't know where that word came from but I wrote it neatly under *Rubik's Cube* in my notebook. He wrote something on the yellow pad, put it in his briefcase and turned his attention to me.

"Why do you ask, Francis?"

"Because I'm curious. I'm here to get answers, right?"

"Fair enough."

I stopped fiddling with my pen and looked into Mr. Bergeron's eyes. That's what my father taught me to do when I was playing poker. I had managed to run the gauntlet of the library and the boys' washroom to get into his office. I might as well cut to the chase. What I asked him next may seem like it came out of the blue, but you have to understand that it was the One Big Question that obsessed me.

"Do you believe in God?"

"Yes," he said.

"Why?"

"That's a good question." He took the Rubik's Cube in his left hand, and pushed a little plastic square with his thumb. "I believe in God because I want to. I want to believe that Something exists, and that Something is bigger than me. And you, do you believe in God?"

"Me? I don't know." While my mother was reading *Theresa of Avila*, at the urging of Aunt Sophie, I was reading Eric's tattered copies of Jean-Paul Sartre and Simone de Beauvoir, neither of whom were big on religion.

"A human being needs to give life meaning, especially his own life. Some people find it through religion while others find it through volunteering, arts, yoga, whatever. It's different for each of us."

I studied the floor. White marble tiles. Bergeron's office had been decorated with stark, modern furniture and apricot walls, as if it had been transported from a glossy magazine and plunked down in our decrepit high-school building.

"Was it my fault?" The words came out of my mouth, surprising me.

"Your father committed suicide. He was the only one responsible."

I hate the S-word. Could he have said it any louder? SUICIDE. Wait a second. I will write it in capital and bold letters, just to be sure I don't forget that my father committed **SUICIDE**.

"Do you feel guilty?" His voice was gentle.

The old sea serpent was waiting in the wings. I tried to keep it down the best I could. I failed. It was awkward and liberating at the same time.

"Yes."

"Why?"

"If I hadn't gone to New York, he couldn't have killed himself."

"Don't you think he would have done it another day?" Silence.

"Don't you think he would have done it anyway?" he said gently. "When you were at school? You couldn't watch him all day, every day. You would have to let him out of your sight. You have a right to live your own life."

I was staring at the Rubik's Cube as if it held the clue to the meaning of the universe.

Mr. Bergeron continued. "You know, it's normal to feel guilty. And it's very good that you expressed it today.

Losing a parent is a shock. A tragedy. You must know that you're not alone. I know plenty of teenagers just like you who've lost a parent. It's normal to feel pain. It's normal to cry. It's normal."

Normal. So, I wasn't a grief freak. I was normal. I wasn't entirely convinced, but I allowed myself to smile at him before leaving his office.

The following week, when I came back to see him, I left my notebook in my locker.

9 | JULIA

We were sitting in a circle on folding metal chairs in a church basement on Côte-des-Neiges, not far from the Université de Montréal campus, on the other side of the mountain. A battered trestle table was set with a paper plate of dry cookies – Fudgee-Os, my favorites – cans of pop, and a battered urn of bitter-smelling coffee. My legs were shaking and my jaw twitched. I was a quivering mess.

It was my first meeting with Mr. Bergeron's support group. There were ten of us between ten and seventeen years old. The ten year old was a tiny Asian girl in a Barbie sweatshirt with pink barrettes in her hair, and I heard the seventeen year old say, "I'll meet you in an hour," as he left his pregnant girlfriend at the doorway. The only thing we had in common was that we were reluctant members of the Lost a Parent Club.

I was surprised to see Julia, the girl from my French class, reading a magazine while she waited for everyone to sit down. I hadn't realized that she had lost one of her parents. I guess it's not the first thing you say when you meet someone new: *Hi! My father killed himself seven months ago. My name is Francis, what's yours?*

Mr. Bergeron led the discussion as if he were a maestro. Maestro. Another juicy word. I wrote it ten times in my notebook so I wouldn't have to look at anyone.

"Good evening, everyone, and welcome. My name is Raymond," he said.

It took me a while to absorb this. Mr. Bergeron had an actual first name just like the rest of the human beings on the planet. I thought for a moment about Mr. Enrique and how much he loved his cat, Rococo. Raymond was wearing a white T-shirt with jeans, and his glasses. He'd wound duct tape around the bridge.

Oh, Lord! He was twirling his Rubik's Cube in his hand. I watched, mesmerized, as he began.

"Welcome, Andrew," he said to the boy beside him. Andrew was about fourteen years old, and was slouched over as if the very act of sitting up required too much energy.

"Hi."

"How was your day?"

"Not so good. I thought about my father all day long. He died ten thousand and eighty seconds ago." He looked around at us as if we were about to contradict him. I didn't want to fish for my calculator so I was grateful when Raymond said,

"Just one week ago."

Andrew started to cry. Raymond reached over and took his hand.

"I'm supposed to go back to school on Monday, but I can't. He's always there, inside my head." The words came out of him ragged and painful. "He had a heart attack and just like that he was gone. Why did it happen?" It was agony listening to him.

Raymond turned to the rest of us. "Why? That's the question we all have, and the question none of us can answer. Perhaps it is not *why*, but *what* we do after that counts."

"I don't want to talk anymore," Andrew whispered. He wiped his eyes on his sleeve.

"It's okay, Andrew. If you don't want to, it's okay."

I remember the week after my father died, and it was awful. The fact of the death filled every part of my mind every single minute of the time. As I listened to Andrew I realized that without noticing it, I had moved beyond that horrible time.

It took an effort, but I raised my hand. It was cold in the church basement and the cookies were doing the cha-cha in my belly.

"Good evening. My name is Francis, and my father died last June." That felt good, but I knew that I had only said half of what needed to be said.

"How did he die?" asked the Barbie girl.

"My father . . . he . . . my father committed suicide. He hanged himself in the attic."

There. I said it. Now everyone knew not only that my father committed suicide, but how he did it. I wanted to get it out before they asked me. People always want the juicy details. It's like:

"Oh! I'm so sorry about your father."

"It's okay."

They wait a second or two, and then:

"How did he do it? Pills, a gun, a screwdriver?"

Stupid idiots. If they were really sorry, how could they possibly ask me that?

The discussion moved on to something else, but I felt like I had taken a giant step. At the end of the evening, as we were folding up the chairs, I actually found the nerve to speak to Julia. This was a big deal for me, let me tell you.

"My name is Francis, but you can call me Frank if you want." Nobody has ever called me Frank, but I thought it sounded cool.

"That goes for me, too." There it was again – the delicate scent of lily of the valley.

"What? You want me to call you Frank?" Ha, ha! Was I hilarious! It's a wonder she didn't run screaming for the door.

Instead she said, "No, sorry. Call me Jul. Actually I hate to be called Julia – and tomatoes."

"Sorry?"

"I hate tomatoes They're squishy and they have those little seeds. I think they're gross."

"Me, too! There's nothing on earth that I hate more than tomatoes!" This was not precisely true. I actually had never taken a stand on the tomato issue, but apparently there's a Talking to Girls Monster that's as independent of rational thought as the Grief Sea Monster. I seemed to have lost all control of my brain.

"But I love Dijon mustard!" I couldn't believe I said that. But anyway, we both laughed. She had warm hazel eyes, brown hair, and best of all, she was shorter than I am. I like girls who are shorter than I, though there aren't many of them. She was also younger. I was born in April, and she was born in October. I liked the way she was handling her soda. So sexy! She had a nice, white toothy smile. Teeth are always the first thing I notice in girls. Well, the second thing. She must have noticed my fixation.

"I had braces for at least five years. My teeth were terrible! I could have given Dracula a scare!" This brilliant conversation went on until the other kids had left and Mr. Bergeron was clearing his throat loudly at the door.

~~~

On meeting nights, I spent hours in my bedroom picking through what you might generously call my wardrobe for my least dorky clothes, and – very important – shaving. I tried to comb my hair like Tom Cruise, and I patted eau de cologne on my face. That was something I'd never done before. I used Papa's because I didn't have money to buy a new bottle. I could never figure out the point of cologne before, but it seemed like a good idea.

The highlight of my week was talking to Jul after Group. We'd take our plate of cookies and our cans of pop and perch on the edge of the dusty stage that ran across one end of the basement. We talked about her mother and my father. What she went through was different from me. I guess every death is different. Her mother died from breast cancer when Jul was eleven. Last year her father sold his construction company in Barrie. Jul went to Paris on a school exchange while her sister and dad moved to Montréal. After that first conversation about tomatoes, no matter where we started we always ended up talking about death. She told me that she had had time to prepare herself for her mother's death, but when it came, it was still a shock. Jul told me that since her mother had died she had more or less stopped eating. I noticed that she hadn't touched the cookies.

You'd think that after that kind of heart-to-heart, talking to Jul at school would be no problem. Wrong. Outside the church basement, Mr. Cool, here, was tongue-tied. It took me ages to psyche myself up, but finally, on a Friday afternoon when classes were over, I asked her to go to Deli Delight with me. The owner's an old potbellied man who wears a skullcap and speaks French with a strong Yiddish accent. He is one of those people that you can know forever, without ever knowing his name. Even Papa, who had known him for years, called him *Mister Deli*. Mr. Deli had been at the funeral.

We slid into a booth and I ordered sodas, tuna salad on bagels, and fries. We picked up the familiar Theme of Death conversation before the food came. Jul began.

"She suffered a lot. I'll never forget every minute of the last day. The nurse came to her room and gave her a shot. An hour later, she was dead. She held my hand till the end. I didn't want to cry in front of her. I didn't cry for the whole two years she was sick."

"Why not?"

"Because I wanted to show her that I was strong and that she wouldn't have to worry about what would happen to me after she was gone. I wanted her to be able to go in peace."

"In a way, you're lucky. You knew your mother was going to die. You could tell her that you loved her. I never got the chance."

"I did say it a lot to her, but I also said stuff I can't believe now. Once, about six months before she died I was mad at her for something. I don't remember what – maybe because I had turned the radio up too loud and she yelled at me. I yelled back that I wished she were dead. I kept thinking about that during the last days when she actually was dying. I'd give anything to take those words back. Then, at the end it was so awful that I wanted my mother to hurry up and get it over with. I really did wish she was dead. It's horrible to say that, isn't it?" Jul studied my face.

I reached across the table for her hand. This incredibly sicko thought formed in my mind. I wanted to become the tears that rolled down her cheek just so that I could touch her skin. I must be a pervert.

"I felt two emotions at the same time," Jul continued. "I wanted my mother to die so that she wouldn't suffer anymore, but at the same time, I wanted her to live, because I loved her and couldn't bear to lose her. Nobody seems to get it."

I didn't say anything. I was beginning to figure out that sometimes listening is the best way to communicate. Some people (like Aunt Sophie) are afraid of silence, so they fill it with sounds. *Don't cry. Cry. You're the Man of the House now. How do you feel? It was all for the best.* Let me tell you, when it's your turn to be a good friend to somebody who is in bad shape, just listen. Forget words. They can be worse than useless.

Mr. Deli brought us our sodas, humming I don't know what – it sounded like "All That She Wants" from Ace of Base. I watched Jul pull the paper wrapper off her straw and take a sip.

"I don't know if it's like this for you," she said, "but I'm jealous of people who have both their parents. You know Reine?"

"Reine Green?"

"Yes. We walk to school together sometimes, and she's always talking about going to buy a dress for her graduation with her mother, and how her mother likes white dresses and what stores she likes and on and on and on. It makes me want to scream. When it's my turn to graduate, I won't be shopping with my mother. My mother's never going to see me graduate or get married, or have kids, or anything."

I thought about my fury at Houston's ongoing saga of *Father Knows Best*. "Yes, but your father and your sister will be there." I don't know why I said that. I had my mother and brother, and that didn't make the pain any less.

"It's not the same at all. I love my father, I really do, but there are things that a girl wants to talk about with her mother."

"I know. It's the same for me."

"Besides, my father never shows his emotions. He's about as warm as the St. Lawrence in January!"

Oh, my God! She said *as warm as the St. Lawrence in January*! I thought I'd made that expression up. We use the same expressions! We were obviously meant for each other.

Mr. Deli arrived with our tuna bagels. Jul picked the sliced tomato off hers, took one or two rabbity bites, and pushed her plate away. When she ran her hand through her hair – even though there was a spot of mayonnaise on her fingertips – I could have melted right then and there.

It won't come as a surprise to you that I asked her my inevitable God question.

"I don't know if I believe in God," she said. "When you die, what do you think happens after?"

"I guess there are two possibilities. Either your body decomposes, becomes fertilizer to feed plants and animals, and that's the end. Or, there's a soul that quits your body and flies into the universe. That's what Maman thinks."

She sat silently. Her face was still.

"What are you thinking?" I said.

"I never thought about death before my mother died. I thought death had to do with other people. I really thought, even if it sounds stupid, that I was immortal."

"It's not stupid, Jul."

"I thought I would never die. The fact that my mother died forces me to accept that I will too."

"Death is a thief. We never know when he will come." Mr. Deli put a plate of french fries in the middle of the table. "Don't let him steal your youth."

Something about the way he said it struck me as comforting. We both looked at him as if he had solved the mystery.

~~~

The days had been growing longer. When I got home, grinning like a demented ad for toothpaste, it was still light. I could hear Sputnik's anxious yips as he waited for Luc to throw his ball in the backyard. Maman was sitting on the front porch sewing a button back on my pants. She had Papa's jacket draped over her shoulders.

"Well, that's done. Here are your pants." She snapped the thread off with her teeth.

"Thanks." I leaned my bike against the railing and sat down beside her.

"Where were you?"

"I was with Jul at the deli."

"I would really like to meet her someday, this Jul. You spend a lot of time with her." She raised her eyebrows and smiled at me expectantly. When I didn't answer she shrugged, closed her sewing box and got to her feet. "We're having fish for dinner."

A moment later I could hear her in the kitchen pulling pans out of the cupboard. She must have turned on the radio because I could hear the low sweet sounds of Fats Domino singing *Blueberry Hill*. She called to Luc through the open window, "Come in and wash up. It's time to eat."

Out of nowhere, I felt the stab of a memory that brought me such a rush of joy I could hardly stand it. It brought back an evening just like this one. Papa had taken me to the park, and we could hear Maman calling from down the street:

"Francis, Ben, it's time for dinner!" When we came in, Maman pretended to be angry. "Ben, for heaven's sake, why did you take Francis to play in the park when you knew dinner was almost ready? Both of you are filthy!"

"Don't worry, *mon amour*, I'll take care of Francis." He tugged her ponytail.

"Your *amour* wants you to change your clothes first. I just finished cleaning the kitchen, and I don't want to have to do it again. Make sure you don't wake up Luc. I just settled him."

"We have our marching orders, *mon amour*." He give her a quick kiss and scooped me up.

Mon amour. That was what my father used to call her. During the long last year, I don't even remember him saying her name.

Papa and I changed our clothes as ordered, because on matters of cleanliness, there was no arguing. Maman kept everything spotless, including me and Luc. When Aunt Sophie said, "You can eat off her floor," which was something she said about one thousand times, Papa would wink at me and say, "Finally, a plate big enough for Sophie!"

⁂

Maman served the fish. She'd snipped some of her potted dill to sprinkle on top. The curtains billowed at the open kitchen window and the air was delicate, if you know what I mean. Maman, Luc, and I sat at the table eating in comfortable silence. That night, my appetite came back without my even noticing.

10 | DINOSAURS

One Sunday night we all went to see *Jurassic Park*. I like Steven Spielberg. The first time I ever went to the movies was when I was five and my parents took me to see *E.T. The Extra-Terrestrial*. I didn't want to cry in front of my parents when E.T. had to leave Eliot, but I couldn't help it.

It wasn't a date, exactly, because my friends were there, but I waited at the ticket counter for Jul so that I could sit beside her. She finally arrived, but she was yakking at an older kid, David, her arm looped through his. I realized that I'd never actually touched her. She gave me a tiny nod but didn't stop talking to him.

There was an empty seat next to Melanie. She can always make me laugh and that night I laughed like a lunatic at everything she said. There's a French expression, so jealous that you lose your teeth. Think about it.

Melanie looks a little like Aunt Sophie, which can be kind of off-putting. I don't mean she's ugly – she's not. It's just that she and Aunt Sophie are the kind of people who take up a lot of room. They both favor eye-aching colors and laugh all the time. What's annoying is that they both laugh at every one of my jokes – not all of which are funny, I'll be the first to admit. I hate it when I make a truly unfunny joke or when I forget the ending of a joke I've heard. I just *hate* that! You know, you're talking, talking, talking, and in the middle, you forget what you wanted to say, but you don't want people to know that you forgot what you wanted to say. You keep talking, talking, talking, and you feel like your brain is about to burst, because you are searching for words, and then you pray that some famous guy will suddenly land right beside you, and everyone will look at him instead of you. But obviously, just when you need famous people they are never there to help you, because they are incredibly selfish. There you are, sweating so hard that you are swimming inside your I ♥ NY T-shirt, that only cost you two dollars, which is so cheap that you bought ten of them to give to your friends, but they had also each bought ten because they are just as cheap as you are (or just as broke), and then you try to distract everyone by pointing to something like the nose of the girl who is seated at your left, and you seize the chance to run in the opposite direction. And you keep running until you become this tiny black spot on the horizon, and that's why they smash you, because they think you are a fly – and then you realize how ridiculous it is to say "He's so kind, he wouldn't hurt a fly," because everyone has smashed a fly at least once in their life, including you.

See how my mind works? I'm twisted. No wonder Jul was sticking her hand into David's bag of popcorn and leaning against his arm. She leaned into his shoulder and whispered something without turning her head. Because of the time she spent in France, she speaks French with a Parisian accent. It would probably get on my nerves in the very near future, but for now I was willing to handle it. If only I got the chance.

After the movie, everybody went off for pizza, but I'd had enough of The Jul and David Lovefest. Besides, my face ached from two hours of enforced hilarity courtesy of Melanie. Instead I went to Deli Delight. The place was empty. By way of greeting, Mr. Deli said, "Fries?" When he brought them he sat down across from me with a loud grunt.

"Your girlfriend didn't come with you?"

"She's not my girlfriend."

"Sorry." Mr. Deli passed me the ketchup bottle and mayonnaise. "Tell me, young man, what do you want to become in life?"

The I'm-Talking-to-a-Kid-and-I-Can't-Think-of-a-Thing-to-Say Question that adults ask.

"I don't know." I did know. I wanted to go to university to study music and then teach people to play. I also knew that it was never going to happen. There was no money. Mr. Deli studied my face. He seemed to have read my mind.

"You're a strong kid. You could take a job to earn some money for your studies. I need some help here. You know, I'm becoming a little bit old. Just a little bit. My eyes are not as good as they were before. Sometimes, I mix up salt and sugar."

"I don't know how to make bagels."

"You can learn. Everything has to be learned in life. Even poker. Your father understood that, you know."

"Did you play with him?"

"Not for a long time. Before I got the deli I had quite a problem with cards. When I had enough money to buy this place, I left the boats and stopped playing. Your father stayed on. You know, your father had a sickness, but he fought it like a gladiator. He was a brave man."

"If he was so brave, why did he abandon my mother, my brother, and me? That's not brave."

"Don't say that. We can't judge others like that."

"Is it your religion that forbids it?" I wasn't asking him for a theology lesson. I was being sarcastic. He didn't notice. Mr. Deli chose his words carefully.

"It is not my religion. It is me. It's something I really believe. You know, in life there are things that we can answer, but others we can't. We have to let go of those things for which we just can't find any answers. We can't hold onto them."

I let the fries grow cold on my plate. I wasn't angry anymore. As I walked home the same thought beat a tattoo with my steps: *Why didn't Papa talk to me? Why didn't we ever talk?*

～

I was twelve years old when I saw my father cry for the first and only time. He was in the garage, sitting on a bench with his toolbox beside him. Maman was baking an apple pie, and we could smell the warm cinnamon.

"Why are you crying, Papa?" I was shocked and afraid.

He didn't answer, he just wept silently. Finally, he raised his head. "I lost my job."

"You'll find another one."

"No." He sounded defeated.

11 | THE MEMORY BOOK

Though we were well into spring, the weather had turned cold again and rain was beating on the window. I hadn't heard from Jul all week. I knew I wasn't much of a prize, compared to David. For starters, I was downright skinny. Though I ate nonstop, gobbling industrial quantities of Fudgee-Os, I was a beanpole.

Luc had finally fallen asleep after four readings of *Simon and the Snowflakes*. I was sitting by his bed listening to his even breathing when I was blindsided by a wave of longing for Papa. I wanted desperately to ask him what you're supposed to do when you're in love with a girl who is so clearly, cruelly, not in love with you.

I closed Luc's door softly and went down to the living room. Maman had a paper pattern spread out on the rug in front of her and was squinting at it and the knitting in her hands.

"You won't be walking around in bare feet for much longer, my boy. I'm knitting wool slippers for you."

"I don't need them, Maman. I'm fine in bare feet."

"So fine that you cough all the time! I don't want you to catch a cold that could become pneumonia. I lost your father. That's enough for me. When I finish these slippers, you will wear them. *Point final*." She was in her element, knitting up the troubles of the world. I watched her struggle with the wool, Papa's vest buttoned over her sweater.

"It's cold in here. Francis. Get another log for the fire. It feels like February. What a crazy year."

I brought another log in from the diminished pile on the front porch, and she patted the couch beside her.

"Tell me, sweetheart, what's happening with Jul? You never talk about her anymore."

"There's nothing for me to say." Oh, Lord, was she going to talk about sex with me?

She lined the knitting needles up carefully on the coffee table. "I can see that there's something wrong. I know you as if I had knitted you. I could tell you each of your stitches, my boy."

She put her arm around my shoulder. The fire was crackling in the fireplace. The clean sharp smell of burning pine filled the room.

"Mr. Deli offered me a job."

"What did you say?"

"Nothing. I said I would think about it. What do you think, Maman?"

"Well, I think it could be a good idea. It would give you some money of your own. You know that with my salary there's not much left over after I've paid for the groceries and such. We'll have to fix the roof soon."

"Did you know that Mr. Deli used to be a sailor? He even worked with Papa."

"Sure. Papa liked him. I used to tell him that Mr. Deli is proof that there's life after the sea, but he wouldn't listen to me."

I don't know where the longing came from but all of a sudden I was desperate to hold a hand of cards with their ordered suits, and sit in the companionable silence of a good game with a good partner. "Maman, let's play cards. Poker."

"My poor boy, I have been knitting all afternoon, and a good part of the evening because I want your feet to be cosy. My eyes hurt. Another time, okay darling?"

❧

I sat on my bed and groped for my guitar. As I did, I knocked my baby album from the shelf above it. I hadn't opened it for years. I wasn't about to unlock a genie all by myself, so I carried it down to the living room, where my mother was watching the fire. I held the album out to her.

"Do you want to look at it?" Her voice was tentative. "I think this calls for a cup of coffee."

I went to put the kettle on. When I came back, I saw a tissue box close to her. The album was blue satin with *Our Baby Francis* neatly embroidered on the cover. That used to mortify me. We sat side by side as she turned the pages.

"Oh, Lord! I was so big when I was pregnant. I gained forty pounds, can you believe it? I thought I was so ugly, but look how gorgeous you were! You weighed ten pounds. Look at this photo. It was your baptism. Grandma wanted to carry you, but you were so heavy. I was afraid she would drop you. And that one: you, and your father on Uncle Ted's Ski-Doo. The sound didn't bother you at all. You could sleep anywhere. That year, there was so much snow that we had to crawl out of the house from the second-floor balcony."

I leaned over her shoulder. There was Papa roaring with laughter, tossing me into the air. Baby me peeking out of Papa's backpack as he rested on his ski poles. With Maman in a bathing suit asleep on a dock somewhere in the Laurentians. There was a picture of me, younger than Luc, with my face buried in Papa's ski-jacketed shoulder because a street corner Santa's ho-ho-ing scared me, and another of me at about twelve. With a finger I reached out and touched Papa's face. He was squinting into the winter sun in front of the house on that Christmas day, with a wiggling puppy Sputnik in his arms. I realized I was smiling.

"Maman?"

"Yes, darling."

"I think it's over between Jul and me." It was a huge relief to say it.

"Talk to me." She took a sip of her coffee.

⇛

I got the idea from Aunt Sophie. She had bustled into the kitchen one Sunday after mass, dressed up in a fringed Mexican poncho, high heels, and a beret, her outfit of choice for taking Luc for the afternoon.

"Coffee?" Maman was sitting cross-legged on the floor, cutting mats out of Sputnik's fur with her manicure scissors. She nodded toward the kettle.

"Of course!" Aunt Sophie settled into a chair with her mug while I gathered together the juice boxes, the pieces of Lego, the miniature cars, the extra sweater, and all the other gear that Luc needed. And no, they weren't out to scale Everest. They were taking the métro to the Biodôme to look at a display on the rain forest.

Aunt Sophie rummaged in her bag and held out a pink teddy bear wearing a knit sweater covered in hearts for Maman to admire. "Isn't he adorable?" she said, giving its black plastic nose a loud kiss.

"Is that yours? Why do you have a bear? Bears are for babies." Luc was suspicious.

"Ah, yes, *mon cher*. It was a gift. Let me tell you, you can keep your diamonds. There's nothing more romantic than a stuffed animal." She gave Maman a knowing look and let loose a volley of laughter.

That's how I came to buy Jul a stuffed monkey, Curious George. I gave it to her on the last night of Group. She seemed pleased about it at the time, almost as pleased as I was for being so utterly smooth.

It didn't actually make a difference. At lunch she handed me a pink envelope with scalloped edges. Inside was a card with a kitten playing with a piece of string. In purple ink, she had written:

> *Thanks for being such a good friend. You're like a brother to me.*

I felt sick.

~~~

"Poor Francis! I'm so sorry."

Maman hugged me. I could feel her delicate bones and I realized how skinny she'd become.

"I told her all kinds of things that really mattered and now she thinks of me as a brother."

"Maybe you could tell her how you feel."

Sure, and maybe I can also take her for a ride in my Ferrari. What's worse, I had already tried, but it hadn't worked out very well.

Maman said, "Poor baby." I hated it when she called me a poor baby. "You know, Francis, you can't force somebody to be in love with you any more than you can be forced to love somebody."

"I love her, Maman. It's the first time I've ever felt anything like this. I really thought she was the one for me."

"You're so young. You'll find somebody else."

That's exactly what I wanted to hear. No, wait – it's exactly what I wanted to hear if I needed a good excuse for murder.

"Why are you so set on her?"

"Because she knows what it's like to have somebody die. Her mother died."

"You don't need to be a chicken to recognize an egg." I could hear the Gospel According to Aunt Sophie. "You'll find somebody who understands you and loves you, even if they haven't gone through the same experiences as you."

I plucked at the wormy green tufts of the rug.

"I seem to lose everyone I love. What's wrong with me?"

She gave a little laugh. "I don't understand a thing about love. All I know is that it's so wonderful that it can make you happy or miserable or even furious. And there's nothing wrong with you. You're just sad."

"I'm sick of being sad." As I said the words, I realized they were true. I stayed on the floor with Maman's arms wrapped around me, not wanting to move. Then I went up to bed.

～

I had grown to dread the long, dark hours when I would lie awake and my thoughts would roar inside my head. Mr. Bergeron had told me that we're programmed to be afraid in the night, so that we stay put in our caves and saber-toothed tigers can't get at us. There were lots of nights when I would rather have faced any beast than the thought of Papa hanging from a rope. That night I dreamed about him, something I hadn't done since he died. In my dream I was walking home when I saw him sitting on the porch waiting for me.

"Papa? Is it you?" I called. "What are you doing here?"

He smiled. "I'm waiting for you so that we can have a game of poker, son. The cards are on the table and I got here in time to clean up the kitchen so that your mother can play with us. It's been a while."

He seemed so solid that I thought I could reach out and touch him.

"Papa?"

"Yes, son."

"I've been waiting for you, too. Did you hear me crying for you?"

He ignored my question. "Hurry up, before the wind blows the cards away. It will be too late then."

As I reached the house, a gust of wind caught the cards and sent them flying up in the air. I grabbed at them, but the wind was too strong. Then, it lifted everything – the cards, the swing that hangs from the maple tree, the house, my father.

I yelled, "Papa, come back! I beg you. You have to stay!"

His voice came to me faintly. "I have to go. I have someone to see. Don't worry, son. I love you."

He vanished and took everything with him, leaving me alone on the sidewalk. A few of the cards drifted down from the sky. There was no other trace of his passage.

⚬⚬⚬

I woke up feeling comforted, as if I'd eaten hot chicken soup on a blustery day. I took my father's chest out of the bottom drawer and reread the scrap of paper.

You have to remember that everything that year had the surreal quality of a dream. It's the only way I can explain what happened next. I was not what you'd call a world traveler: the only time I'd been away from Montréal by myself was the school trip to New York, and going with classmates and teachers is hardly what you'd call alone. That'll give you an idea of how farfetched this sounds. I decided I was going to go to the poker reunion. All the while, the tiny part of my brain that was thinking clearly was asking questions: *How was I going to get to Toronto? What would I use for money? Where would I stay?* I ignored these. All the while I was making plans, I knew it was crazy, but deep down, I hoped that Papa would be there.

12 | CLEAN-UP

"What's up with your house?" Houston had his headphones on as we walked home from school so his voice boomed. I looked up the street and could see that the front door and all the windows were flung wide open.

I left Houston behind and ran, my heart throbbing in my chest, and pounded up the steps.

"Take off your shoes this instant! I just washed the floor." Maman was dressed in a torn Grateful Dead T-shirt and shorts, her hair tucked under a baseball cap. She was on her hands and knees polishing the floor with wood soap.

"And stay away from the walls, they've just been scrubbed."

"Why? They looked fine to me."

"The house was due for a cleaning. After I'm through here, you and I are going to attack the attic."

The attic. No way. "I'm not setting foot in it."

"Did you hear me, Francis? You have to help me." She leaned back on her heels and wiped her hands on her shorts.

"Why? You're the one who wants to go up there, not me."

"Don't start."

I looked around the living room. Cardboard boxes from the liquor store were piled on the dining room table and in the hall. They had been packed and labeled.

"Papa's clothes?" I asked.

"Yes. Uncle Ted's coming around to pick them up," she said firmly.

"You're giving everything away?"

"I have enough souvenirs of your father in my head. I need to clean up."

"But maybe I'll fit into them someday."

"I put away his favorite T-shirts and his good sweaters for you and Luc. The rest of the stuff will never fit you. You're a skinny one."

Skinny. Hey, I hadn't noticed. I was so skinny that if you shone a flashlight at me you could see the light through my body.

"Don't be a baby. You're sixteen now. You're old enough to understand."

⚬⚬⚬

Sweet Sixteen. I had turned sixteen on April 13, and it was, to say the least, nonfestive. The only thing I knew was that I didn't want a party with my friends. The ol' Grief Monster wasn't tamed enough for me to be sure it wouldn't show up, an unwelcome guest, so in the afternoon we visited Grandpa at the nursing home and spent forty-five long minutes listening to him call me Ben while we fed him a carrot muffin. Sputnik sat expectantly at his feet in anticipation of the inevitable crumbs. Mom had invited Uncle Ted and Aunt Sophie for supper. Uncle Ted didn't show up, but Aunt Sophie did. Maman made lasagna, my favorite food. Aunt Sophie gave me the new U2 CD. I kissed her and her explosion of laughter actually made me smile. Luc gave me a drawing of Sputnik. Papa's birthday was April 14th, and Maman had always baked a cake for us with both our names on it. That year, his name was not there. Mine took up all the space.

It was one of those yo-yo days when I went from feeling okay to zoning out to feeling happy. Aunt Sophie left around seven. *Look Who's Talking* was on TV she wanted to watch it. So ended my big day.

～

"Francis, did you hear me? Yoo-hoo! Where are you? Francis? I'm talking to you."

"About what?" With a snap I came back to the living room smelling of lemony soap. "Throwing out my father's things?"

I slammed out of the house and coasted on my bike down the steep street to Deli Delight.

Mr. D. was pouring coffee at a table where four old men were shoveling in eggs and fried onions and having a full-volume enthusiastic argument that had to do with a racehorse. When Mr. Deli saw me he put down the pot and came over.

"I have exactly what you need."

He brought me a cup of coffee and sat down on the stool beside me. The old men were wrapped up in stories of bets gone wrong and paid no attention to us.

"What's wrong with your eyes?"

"Nothing."

"So, what?"

What's wrong? Let's see. Everything. Feeling like a prize dork about Jul. Being scared that my mother would crack apart and vanish like Papa. Worrying about Luc who seemed happier playing catch with Sputnik than being with kids his own age. Having been such a disappointment that my father didn't think it was worthwhile to stick around while I grew up. I wanted to run, the farther away the better.

"My mother wants to give my father's clothes to my uncle Ted. What's he ever done for us? Now he's going to have Papa's vest and even his shoes. There's nothing left for me."

"I see."

"And she even wants to clean up the attic."

"Sometimes it's good to clean up. We have to brush away the cobwebs."

"You don't understand." Mr. D. waited while I furiously stirred sugar into my cup. "I'm scared of the attic."

I didn't know how to say it. I didn't know how to spit out the words that were choking me.

"It's where Papa died."

Mr. D. nodded in silence. I wanted to cry but instead I said, "Have you ever been to Toronto?"

"Sure. We used to sail down the St. Lawrence with all kinds of cargo." Mr. D. looked at me suspiciously. "Why do you ask?"

"No reason. Have you ever heard of a place called The Sailor?"

He laughed. "Oh, that takes me back." He shook his head as if to rattle a memory loose. "What are you getting at?"

"Do you know the password?"

"Fellows, it's time to close up." Mr. Deli got up and started clearing the old men's table. I knew he wasn't going to answer me.

13 | DELI DELIGHT

I was sitting on a stool in the deli's dingy basement kitchen, peeling potatoes for pancakes and french fries. Upstairs the deli was packed. It was hot, and I was sweating.

"Are you done with the potatoes?" Mr. D. called down the stairs.

"I've got six or seven more to do."

"Leave them for now, and come on up and give me a hand."

I can't say I liked working at the deli, but the money wasn't bad and Mr. D. let me pick the music for the tape recorder that was always on. I brought in Jacques Brel and U2.

"Francis, go serve the man at the table by the window."

"But I've never served anyone!" Talking to strangers was not high on my list of skills. My face burned as a I flipped open the little order pad and asked the man what he wanted to have.

"A clubhouse sandwich and make the bacon well-done." He said without looking up from his newspaper.

"I'm sorry, we don't have any bacon here."

"Is this a deli or what?"

"Yes, but it's a kosher deli. Dairy."

"Shit!"

The man took his newspaper, and left.

"What happened?" Mr. D. asked.

"He wanted a club sandwich."

Mr. D. just shrugged and said, "Finish the potatoes."

It was something like thirty degrees outside – freakishly hot for the month of May. I was soaked by the time I rode home up the mountain. Despite the heat, Maman was humming happily at the kitchen table, repotting her herbs into bright red ceramic pots. She had opened all the windows, but the house still smelled of fresh paint. In the last week she had painted the living room, the kitchen, and all the rooms in the house, except mine. I wanted to keep my room the way it was, pure white. There was color everywhere else – yellow in the kitchen, blue in the living room, and green in the bathroom. She had also cleaned up the attic with Aunt Sophie. I couldn't do it. *Point final.*

❧

In old movies, they show you that time has passed by having the pages fly off a calendar. Without my noticing, the pages that marked the year were disappearing. Maman was happy more often than she was sad. She had left the post office and had gone to work in an architect's office, cheerfully organizing things to her heart's content. She was earning more money and sometimes she went out with Aunt Sophie for a drink or to the movies while I baby-sat Luc. My little Luc. I picked him up at day care yesterday and as I was admiring a fingerpainting he'd done he said, out of the blue, "I think that Papa is really dead now." He hadn't talked about Papa for ages, so he caught me off guard.

"What makes you say that?"

He'd obviously given this a lot of thought. "Because he didn't come for your birthday. He's dead for good. Can we have pancakes for supper?"

⚮

The hard days were getting farther apart, so when they came they surprised me. I was hanging around in the boys' washroom waiting for a break in hall traffic so I could go to see Mr. Bergeron when I was hit by a memory. Papa and I were up on Mont-Royal. He pointed at the tallest oak. "See that tree? It's dying. Even the tallest trees die some day. They go back in the soil and feed the others."

I talked about it with Raymond – Mr. Bergeron. "Was that his way of telling me he was going to die too? Was he asking me for help, but I didn't realize it?"

"Maybe he was just telling you about trees," said Mr. Bergeron.

~

"Knock me over with a feather." That's what Papa would have said, relishing the news. It seemed that Aunt Sophie had met a man. He was a widower, and he didn't have children, but he had a fat, bad-tempered dachshund. Aunt Sophie brought the man and Spaetzle, the dog, over for Sunday dinner. This event could have won the Horrible Family Dinners Derby hands down.

The whole time, I was afraid to catch Maman's eye because I knew that once we started laughing we would never be able to stop. First, there was the fact that Luc had never seen Aunt Sophie with a man before and he gawped unselfconsciously as she fussed away at him like a southern belle. If she'd had a lacy handkerchief, I'm sure she would have fluttered it. Then there was the malodorous dachshund panting under the table, having commandeered all of Sputnik's toys between his stubby paws. On top of that, there was the man himself. When he took off his green baseball cap, I recognized him as the guy who'd ordered the club sandwich at the deli. I don't know if he remembered me or not. It was the first time that a man, other than my father, had eaten at our table. The evening was a mess. A few months ago it would have made me angry or sad. Now it made me laugh.

14 | REPLACEMENT

I woke up with a start to the sound of Luc crying. I found him lying on his bedroom floor – he must have fallen out of bed.

"Can I sleep with you? I'm scared." When I knelt down to rock him, I could feel his fragile body trembling in my arms. Saber-toothed tigers. By the time I had settled him in my bed, he was asleep again.

The next day was Monday. Have I mentioned that on my Hit Parade of Hates Monday mornings are right up there? I poured Luc's cereal into his bowl. Maybe it was the influence of Raymond, but I was on a talking kick. *Talk about things. Don't hide them.*

"What happened last night?" I said.

"A nightmare." He was pressing down on each Cheerio, one after the other, to try to sink it in his milk.

"Really?"

"Nightmares are not funny, Francis," he said sternly.

"No. They're not." I waited.

"I had a dream," he said.

"Was it a nice dream?"

"No," he said in a sharp voice.

I kept excavating for words from him. It was hard work. "What was the dream about?"

"A candy dream."

"You dreamed of candy, and it was a nightmare? That's hard to believe!"

"But it's true! I dreamed I was hungry, and there was nothing I could eat in the house, except for SpaghettiOs. I thought maybe there could be at least some jelly beans in the jar, but there were none."

"What did you do?"

"I cried."

"Why didn't you eat SpaghettiOs?"

"Because I wanted to eat candy. Not SpaghettiOs." He looked up at me to make sure that I understood.

～

After school I did a shift at the deli. Mr. D. was in what was, for him, a talkative mood. "I'm happy to see you. There's a ten pound bag of potatoes with your name on it, my son!"

My son. The words made me want to cry. I went down the narrow wooden steps to the basement and took up my post, peeling spuds, glad to be alone. It was safe down there, with no one to tell me to do my math homework or to nag at me to eat or to ask me to go to the convenience store to buy some milk. When I was done peeling the potatoes, I hauled them upstairs and started to fry them. That is hot work, let me tell you. The green-hat man came back, and this time he asked for a bagel with fries. When I served him, he looked at me in a funny way. He left me five bucks for a tip. I couldn't believe it. Usually, it's a loony – or a toony when it's Aunt Sophie, or Maman – that people give me.

Maman had started going to the hairdresser on Saturday mornings, so I was alone with Luc. I planted him in front of the TV while I cleaned up the kitchen. He was sitting cross-legged on the floor with his plate balanced on his lap, making a mountain of buttery toast crumbs as he stared at Bugs Bunny.

"What's up, Doc?" he said when I came to get his plate. "I want jelly beans!"

"You just had breakfast. If Maman says its okay, you can have some later."

"I want them right now! Later, it's going to be too late."

"Knock it off. You can't have everything you want right now."

He turned back to the TV and I spread out the comics on the floor.

"Can you be my father?" His voice was matter-of-fact, as if he had given the proposition a great deal of consideration. Be his father. Me. I wanted to shake sense into him, and at the same time, I wanted to fold him in my arms.

"We can't replace people just like that. You can't replace a father. *Point final.*"

Luc turned off the TV, and went into the backyard. I was listening to him throwing the Frisbee for the dog when I realized something. I had said *point final.* I sounded like Maman. Heaven help me.

The phone rang. It was Aunt Sophie.

"Hi Francis, is your mother there?"

"No, but she'll be back around noon. She's getting her hair done."

"Oh, of course."

"Aunt Sophie?"

"Yes."

"I'm happy for you. He's a lucky guy."

"Why, Francis, what a sweet thing to say!" I could tell she was surprised. "I met him at the coffee shop between eating doughnut number two and doughnut number three. But he's not my boyfriend." She laughed.

"What happened? Did you break up?" When you're a champion laugher like Aunt Sophie, the delivery and the

message are two separate things. She could be announc-
ing the end of the world for all I could tell from the gusts
of laughter.

"No! We never went out together! He wants to know
your mother. That's why I brought him for dinner. He
likes her. I think she likes him, too."

The words hit me like cold water in the face. Freaking
icy water.

It all made sense: the hairdresser, the good mood, and
the clean-up. *My Mother Had a Boyfriend!* I didn't want to
believe it. It couldn't be. Not Maman. Not already. How
could she dare?

I hung up the phone without saying goodbye. I wanted
to gouge all that fresh paint and smash the cheery red
pots of herbs to the floor. I wanted to yell until the roof
shook. She should have waited. It hadn't even been a year.

I left Luc with strict orders to stay right where he was
until I got back.

"Where are you going?"

"I'm going to grab a bite to eat."

"But you just ate," he said accusingly. "Francis, did a
bee sting you?" Luc had once been stung and now he
used it as a measure of all things awful. It shows you how
upset I must have seemed to him.

"Not just a bee, a bumblebee. A seven-foot-tall monster
bee! Promise me you won't move!"

~

Deli Delight wasn't officially open because it was Saturday, but when I looked inside I could see Mr. D. sitting at the counter, reading the racing form. The door was unlocked.

"What's happened, my boy?"

"Don't call me your boy. You're not my father."

"Ok! It's true, you're not my boy. But I like to call you that anyway." He turned back to the paper.

"It's my mother."

"What's wrong with her?" He was concerned.

"She's got a boyfriend."

With a sigh, Mr. Deli turned on his stool to face me.

"You know, your mother is a young woman. It's possible she will find someone else to share her life."

When he said that, I felt sick. "Yes, but not already!" I said.

"It's true, it's quite early, but life goes on. Your father may be dead, but you have to continue to live, your little brother too. And your mother."

I understood the words as he said them, and if he'd been talking about someone else's mother I might have agreed. But I couldn't stand the idea.

When I got home Maman was in the kitchen unpacking bags of groceries. Her back was to me. I could see that her hair had been streaked a pale blonde.

"Aunt Sophie called," I said.

"Do you know what Luc was doing when I got home?" She didn't turn to face me. Oh, God, I had forgotten all about him. *Just let him be okay and I'll accept any man*

Maman drags in. I'll be the best man at their wedding and never say a word.

"He was playing with a lighter and the cedar branches." She loved the smell of cedar and had placed some branches in a jar on the dining room table. "He could have set the house on fire. Where were you? If something had happened, it would have been your fault!"

"How can you say that? Why weren't *you* here taking care of him like a normal mother?"

She wheeled around. "You have never talked to me like that and you are not going to start today, do you hear me?"

"I know all about it. You should be ashamed!"

"What are you talking about, Francis?"

"Aunt Sophie told me everything."

"Told you what?"

"That you're going out with a man."

Her face flushed an angry red.

"That's none of your business! As long as you live in my house, you'll respect your mother. Get out of my sight!"

I lay on my bed, staring at the blank white ceiling, my thoughts lurching along like a roller-coaster car that's out of control. *Respect?* My mother was a slut who went out with the first man who came along. It wasn't enough that she had me and Luc. If Papa were here, he would never have allowed it. But he wasn't here, and never would be here again. I had to face the truth. He had left me because I wasn't worth sticking around for. No wonder Jul took off. How much can I matter if my own father doesn't want to see me grow up? I'm ugly. I'm skinny. At work I'm worth seven dollars an hour. At school I'm worth 51 percent in math. If I'm not worth anything, I should just die like my father. If I died tomorrow, who would come to my funeral? Would Julia come? Would she cry? Would she feel guilty? Would she come alone, or with her idiot, David? Would my mother come alone, or with her damn boyfriend in his stupid green cap? One thing I knew for certain. Mr. D. would be there, just like he was for my father's funeral. He would cry too. I'm sure.

I went into the bathroom, opened the medicine cabinet, and found the aspirin bottle. It was almost full. I wondered if dying would hurt. If Papa could do it, so could I. Like father like son. I looked at the bottle for a very long time. The label read EXTRA STRONG. I opened the top.

Luc knocked at the door.

"I need to pee! Hurry up!"

That kid was always having to pee! I snapped the top on the aspirin, put it back on the shelf, and opened the door.

"All yours, kiddo." I knew that I could never do it. I wasn't going to make my innocent little brother suffer like Papa had made me suffer. *Point final.*

15 | GREEN HAT

The Anniversary came and went. Maman went to church and to the cemetery, but we didn't talk about it at home. We had slipped back into No Talk/No Pain Mode. The summer yawned ahead. I was looking forward to two steaming months cooped up in the Deli Delight, peeling potatoes for Mr. D. Houston was going on a tour of North American baseball parks with his father, and the others were working as counsellors at a camp in the Laurentians. Luc was enrolled in Dinosaur Day Camp, and Maman was deeply, disgustingly, "involved." Green Hat had taken root, on a more or less permanent basis, in our house.

It was a very hot day, so hot that Maman had turned on the air conditioner. Let the Good Times Roll! This was a sure sign that better financial times had come. Green Hat was sitting on the couch, his knobby, furry legs splayed out in cut-off jeans – disgusting! He and Maman were beaming at each other the way only mentally challenged people can do. She had on a red shirt – too tight for her. She had lipstick all over her face – well, only on the lips, but there was too much of it. I was obviously invisible to them, even though I was standing right there. She leaned toward him and gave him a kiss.

The poor idiot – Green Hat – had tried to win us over. What a dunce! That morning he had brought me an electric guitar. Here's what happened:

"Francis?" It was my mother's voice.

"What do you want?" I was lying on my unmade bed, staring at the ceiling and estimating the number of potatoes I would have peeled by September.

"Can we come in?"

We? She opened the door a crack.

"Look what George has for you!" she said brightly.

George. He had a first name. What kind of dumb name is George? Curious George. What normal woman would call her child George?

"Your mother told me you play guitar. I thought that maybe you'd like to have this," said George. He held out a gorgeous pearlized blue electric guitar.

I had a weak moment. There's no other explanation for what I said next: "Okay. Put it on the desk. I'll take a look at it later."

Maman gave me a look I hadn't seen since she caught me trying to bite Luc when he was a baby. They backed out of the room as if I was rabid. It was a nice guitar, though. I have to admit it.

~~~

I had nagged at Papa to buy me an electric guitar. He told me that it was important to learn acoustic first, and I knew he was right, but I also knew he didn't have the money for a new instrument. Here was George, just handing me an electric guitar as if he didn't have a care in the world about what it cost. If Papa'd had enough money, he wouldn't be dead today. Freaking money. Dirty money. People run after money. People would do anything to get more money, or enough money to live on. Tears coursed down my cheeks, but I was too furious to brush them away.

I didn't notice that Luc had come in until he waggled a Cookie Monster puppet in my face.

"Look what George gave me!"

The puppet was on his right hand. Under his left arm he held a shiny red dump truck, its tipper full of Smarties. He was grinning so hard he looked demented.

"You are nuts!"

"I am not!"

"Retard! Can't you see what he's doing? Green Hat's trying to buy us. He doesn't care about you. He only wants Maman. He's trying to steal her from us!"

Luc's big blue eyes filled with tears and his lower lip quivered. I was glad. I'd found the magic words. I knew that Luc was afraid that Maman would leave like Papa did.

"You have to be careful, Luc. If George gives you presents, we're in trouble."

Looking back, the ugly Grief Serpent must have swallowed my heart. Poor Luc. He bought it. I hated myself for hurting him but I couldn't stop.

Luc's slight shoulders drooped as he went back to his room, carrying his truck and his puppet as if they each weighed a ton. I picked up the guitar and went downstairs. I heard the lovebirds rattling pans in the kitchen, so I went out the front door and down the alley to the garage. It had a stale smell of mice and dust. I laid the guitar on the workbench, grabbed a hammer and swung at its slick blue surface. *BANG. BANG. BANG.* I took the scissors, and I cut every string. I found the hand drill and I made a hole in its body.

Sputnik planted his paws in the open door and barked at me as if I were a stranger.

"Francis, what are you doing, *mon cher?* Is everything okay?"

"I'm in the garage." She must have been dazzled by Green Hat's charms not to have worried about the murderous noises I was making.

"Well, it's time to eat. Come in."

I could barely stand to look at Green Hat. I wanted to scratch his face with the fork I was holding tightly in my right hand. I wanted to cram it into his throat and choke him. I needed a human sacrifice badly. I felt as if all my pain and anger and fear had taken on the shape of this one man.

I didn't say a word during supper. I was looking at my plate.

"What did you do today, sweetheart?"

"Lots of things."

"Such as?"

I had read once that a human being breathes 840 times an hour. It was about 7 p.m.

"I breathed about 15,900 times. That's what I did today."

For dessert I went and got the guitar corpse from the garage. I put it on the table, beside the chocolate cake. I stormed upstairs, knowing that I was acting like a colossal jerk, but feeling free just the same. I could hear Luc yelling at Green Hat:

"You're mean! You want to steal my Maman!"

⚉

I heard footsteps and then the creak of my door opening. No polite knocking this time.

Maman marched in. "For God's sake, what did you say to Luc?" She looked like Alice Cooper, her makeup smeared all over her face. "Why are you acting this way? Francis? Answer me!"

I didn't understand why, I just knew that I was in a rage. Her mascara had made black football player smudges under her eyes.

"Why are you so mean, Francis?"

"I am not mean. *You* are!"

"Why can't I have a little bit of happiness?"

"What about Luc and me?"

She clasped her hands to her head and repeated softly, "Why can't I have a little bit of happiness?"

I felt that the air had been knocked out of me. "It's only been a year, Maman. Only one year."

"I've cried enough, I think." Her voice had grown calm and cool and it enraged me.

"How dare you replace him like that, with freaking Green Hat?"

"His name is George! Stop calling him Green Hat!"

"You can't replace Papa."

"I don't want to." Her composure vanished and she collapsed on my bed, curled up on her side, and cried like a baby.

I don't know how long we were frozen in place, but eventually she sat up. I handed her a Kleenex and she snuffled. "You know, I'm really angry with your father. He cut out and left me with no money and two kids to raise alone."

"You're not alone, Maman. I'm here with you."

"I know, but it's not the same thing, Francis. Someday, when you fall in love, you will understand what I'm talking about."

Huh! Falling in love. I wasn't about to do that again. I'd learned my lesson.

"Okay," she sounded defeated. "I understand it's only been a year. I will ask George to leave. But listen to me very carefully: I'm doing this because of *you*. It's the first and last time in my entire life I'll do this. Do you *hear* me? The first and last time. Now, I don't think I want to talk to you for a while." She closed the door and left me alone.

⁓

The day after the Leaving of Green Hat, Aunt Sophie appeared at the deli. It was around six on Monday evening. There were only two or three customers sitting at the back. Mr. Deli was in the basement fretting over the bagel oven. The Cranberries were playing on the radio. It was raining softly.

Aunt Sophie shook out her umbrella and sat on a stool at the counter so she could talk to me while I sliced potatoes. "Your mother told me everything," she said. She looked like a big potato herself, in her wrinkled linen dress with her face drawn into unaccustomed lines. I concentrated on the cutting board.

"I'm disappointed in you. If I were you, I wouldn't be proud of me," she said.

The more I agreed with her inside, the madder I got. When you're already beating yourself up for doing something stupid, you don't need anyone else's help. Aunt Sophie had always been in my corner. I didn't want to feel ashamed in front of her.

"You aren't me!" I was yelling without meaning to.

She leaned across the counter. "Look at me, Francis."

I clenched my fist. "You're dumber than this potato and I hate you." I heaved the potato at the window. Luckily I hit the newspaper rack.

"You're crazy, just like your father!" Aunt Sophie stood and shook her umbrella at me.

I guess at that minute I was. I started chucking all the potatoes I'd peeled at the door. She left. The three customers sat looking at me. Mr. Deli came huffing up the stairs.

"What are you doing? You can't throw potatoes like that! You can't do that!" Mr. Deli looked at me as if I had three heads. He unfolded a green garbage bag and started picking up the potatoes. "Violence begets more violence!"

"Oh, great. More words of wisdom."

Mr. D. didn't look angry so much as confused. And disappointed.

I had clearly cracked. Mr. Reptile Brain had taken over in my skull. I had managed to terrify Luc, wreck Maman's plans, and alienate both Aunt Sophie and Mr. D. Good going, Francis! A triple-header. No, a quadruple-header. No wonder Papa couldn't stand me.

～～～

I washed my face at the tiny sink in the men's room and left the deli. It was raining so hard that I took off my T-shirt. I walked down St-Denis and turned on Mont-Royal.

I didn't stop until I came to the big statue of an angel at the entrance to the cemetery. She looked as if she was giving me a high five. Everything was clear in my mind. I had to leave.

～

Aunt Sophie had loaded Luc and Sputnik into her car and taken them to a holiday camp in the Laurentians for a week. Maman and I had hardly exchanged a word since the End of the Affair. I had convinced myself that nobody would miss me if I left.

～

August 14, 1993. My own private D-Day. I was going to fly on my own wings, but, truth be told, I felt more like Tweety Bird than an eagle. After I bought my bus ticket I had two hundred and fifty dollars in potato-peeling money sorted neatly in my brand-new wallet. My knapsack was packed with a couple of bottles of Pepsi, my Walkman and tapes, some underwear, a couple of T-shirts, and a map of Toronto.

I took the métro to Berri-UQAM. From there, it was only a five-minute walk to the bus station, but I was drenched with sweat as I stood in line for a ticket. Part of my brain knew that what I was doing was not the brightest of moves, but it was overruled by the litany of reasons I had assembled to convince myself that I had to go: I wanted to leave all the pain, frustration, anger – wait a second, where's my synonym dictionary? Okay. Just found it – disappointment, fury, rage, resentment, and bitterness behind me. I also had plenty that I wanted to forget. For instance, there was making a fool of myself over George, and telling Jul that I liked her. But most of all, I wanted to forget that Papa hadn't loved us enough to stick around. Those were the *push* reasons. The *pull* reason was Password: Black Jack.

16 | THE SAILOR

The bus was nearly full. I sat down in an aisle seat next to an old woman in a pink pantsuit with soft white hair and glasses on a beaded cord. Before the bus pulled out of the station she told me that she was from Barrie, Ontario, and that she was on her way home from visiting her granddaughter. I wondered if she knew Jul, but I had a horror of speaking to strangers so I didn't ask. I slept until the bus stopped at Kingston. There was a Tim Hortons there, and though I wasn't hungry I bought a turkey sandwich. The old woman gave me an apple.

"Where are you going, dear?" she asked.

"Toronto." Ever the snappy conversationalist, me.

"Do you have family there?"

"No."

"Is this your first visit?"

"Yes." Was she never going to stop asking me questions?

"Lord, Lord, you'll enjoy yourself. You know the Exhibition is on. My, it's fun, what with the roller coaster and the midway. There's the Food Building. My, I used to love going to see Elsie the Cow carved out of butter, but now it's all . . ."

"Excuse me." I got up and lurched down the aisle to the minuscule washroom to get away from her. I came back to my seat, hoping that the Inquisition was over. It wasn't.

"Are you from Montreal?"

"Yes."

"Do you like it?"

"Yes." I was going to have to jump off this bus. I didn't care if it was speeding down a highway. I chose the only other option. Lurch down the aisle to the washroom again, and when the smell got to be too much, lurch back to my seat.

"How old are you, dear?"

"I'm sixteen."

"Oh, my dear! Sixteen! If only I could be sixteen once again with all the experience I have, dear! Life would be so cool!"

Cool? I'd never heard an old lady use that word. Weird.

"Do you have a girlfriend?"

What kind of person was this? The source of my profound knowledge of the citizens of Barrie was Jul, and she had led me to believe that they were normal. Not if this lady was an example. She was odd, strange, and if I hadn't written the word *weird* three lines up, I would have used it again here. What was strange about her was not the persistent questioning, but the fact that I somehow felt compelled to answer. I had never needed to be told "don't talk to strangers." *Shy* was my middle name. By some magical force, she had me spilling my guts.

"I used to, but it's over now. She was *verboten*."

Verboten. I had no idea what the word meant, but I liked the way it sounded so I used it whenever I wanted to make an impression.

"Oh . . . I'm sorry." She sounded puzzled. "You know, I had my first boyfriend when I was sixteen. I ended up marrying him, and we were married for seventeen years. Then he died." She smiled at the memory, as if she were skipping over the *died* part.

"I'm sorry."

"Thank you, my dear. He's been gone a great many years, now. Do you have brothers and sisters?"

"Just my little brother."

"I only had the one child, my daughter. She was nine when her father died. It was a long time ago."

I held the foil-wrapped turkey sandwich out to her.

"How kind of you. Don't mind if I do." She took half.

"My father died too," I said.

"Oh. I'm sorry to hear that. What happened to him?"

"Sorry, I have to go to the washroom."

My hands were wet. I went to the washroom once again, but eventually I had to leave the fetid little cubicle because someone was pounding on the door. Besides, the old lady was a perfect stranger. I would probably never see her again.

I sat back down beside her and said, "My father committed suicide."

"My poor boy."

No surprise there. Everyone always said that when they heard the news. Poor boy, poor Francis, poor whatever.

"Do you want to know how he died?" I said. I wanted to head her off at the pass.

"Only if you want to talk about it."

"He hanged himself in the attic."

She didn't say anything, just looked out the window at the cars speeding in the opposite direction. I wasn't sure that she had heard me.

"That's not all. Do you want to know something else?"

"Well," she hesitated, but there was no stopping me.

"His neck was so swollen that they could only keep the coffin open for a few minutes. Is there anything else I should tell you?" I realized I was almost shouting, my hands gripping the arms of the seat.

"I'm sorry," she said.

I didn't want to cry, so I concentrated on the bus ceiling, forcing myself to keep my eyes as wide open as possible. That's what I usually do when I know I'm going to cry, but I don't want to. It sometimes works.

"You must be very sad." She put her hand on mine. "Let me tell you something. My husband did the same thing. He committed suicide too. Funny, isn't it, how one person being gone can make the whole world seem so empty."

The bus arrived right on time at seven-thirty in the evening. I carried her bag to the platform where her bus was due to leave for Barrie. We kissed goodbye, and she fished a small box of raisins out of her handbag.

"Raisins are good for you. They give you lots of energy. Take them with you," she said, "and take care." I waited until she was on her bus and waved until it disappeared.

I unfolded my map of Toronto and looked for Chester Street. It was south, close to Lake Ontario. I reckoned it must be near the docks. I hoisted my backpack and walked over to Yonge Street. I asked a kid with a Mohawk and a lip stud if he could point me south. The only thing I knew about Yonge Street is that it's supposed to be the longest street in the world. I believe it. The early evening was so hot and airless that every step I took felt like a mile. From the map it seemed that Toronto was pretty easy to figure out: streets were north-south, east-west – easier than Montréal. I could always orient myself by looking for the CN Tower.

I had folded Papa's note and put it in my wallet.

August 14, 1953. We, the Loyal Order of the Companions of Poker, pledge to meet on August 14, 1993 at 9 p.m.

for a rematch at The Sailor, 142 Chester Street, Toronto.
Password: Black Jack.

I had less than two hours to find The Sailor. You've probably already figured this out, and I hate to admit it, but I may be the most gullible person in the Western world. I was probably the oldest kid on the planet to believe in Santa Claus, and I was shaky on the issue of the Tooth Fairy until Houston set me straight in third grade. Maybe my gullibility – call it my desire to believe – accounts for the fact that I had convinced myself that I would see my father again. There's no other rational explanation.

It was almost eight o'clock, and the sun was fading. According to the map, 142 Chester Street was within walking distance. I bought a hot dog from a vendor, opened a Pepsi, and headed south. I walked and I walked and I walked. I didn't notice the Eaton Centre, the clusters of street people, the traffic. That gives you an idea of how single-minded I was. I had convinced myself that my father was going to be at The Sailor playing poker, and if I could just get there, I'd see him again.

I was almost there. Chester was a street of small tired shops – a dollar store with plastic purses and rubber sandals in the window, a convenience store with a window full of lottery signs, a travel agency offering money orders, and a clothing store with a rack of gaudy T-shirts out in front – and apartments above. There was a rottweiler tied to a parking meter in front of the convenience store, but other than that the street was empty. Beside a bank at 100 Chester Street I found a small patch of yellowing grass with two wrought iron benches. A small sign declared it a *parkette*. One of the benches was occupied by a figure asleep under a newspaper. I was a bit early so I sat on the other bench. Every part of me was in motion. I tapped my fingers and wiggled my feet and shook my legs. That was nothing compared to the contortions my stomach was doing.

I had rehearsed the questions I wanted to ask him:

How did you know you had fallen in love with Maman?
How old were you when you had your first girlfriend?
Were you popular at school?
Were you proud of me?
Why did you leave us?
What's it like to be dead?
Are you happy now?
Can you see me?
Can you hear me?

When I got to the point where I thought I might shake myself apart, what with all my jiggling, tapping, and twitching, I stood up and I walked down the street, squinting to see the numbers above the stores. The sky had grown darker with heavy clouds and the wind was up from the lake.

142 Chester Street. There were beer signs in the windows and a sign that said *Saloon* over one of the doors and

Ladies over the other. The building had been a bar, all right, but it was clearly abandoned, and had been for a long time. It wasn't a bar anymore. It was nothing.

I saw myself vividly: a short skinny boy who looked younger than sixteen, with a school knapsack on his back, standing on a forgotten street hundreds of miles from home. What an idiot I was! What a stupid idiot! What a *freaking* stupid idiot!

The nutty sense of purpose that had propelled me through the day had evaporated and I didn't know what to do. It was beginning to rain. I peered in through the filthy window in the door and I tested it. It gave. I slipped inside. The only light came from a streetlamp outside the window and a neon sign next door that flashed *Shawarma*. It smelled of dust, wood. Cedar. I heard a sound. A rat? Then a cough. I wheeled around, peering into the darkness. Had I imagined it? There was nothing there.

Another cough. I turned again, trying to find its source. My teeth were chattering. There was a flash of lightning and a huge crash of thunder. The room was briefly illuminated. White. I saw the figure of a man. "Papa!"

It wasn't Papa. It was Mr. Deli. He was sitting on a wooden chair in the middle of the empty room. I could hardly make him out in the fading light.

"What are you doing here?" I said.

"Your mother called me this morning to ask me if you were at work. When you didn't turn up, I figured out where you were and I drove down to get you. That's some drive, I can tell you. People are maniacs. So, what's the password?"

A fresh breeze was blowing through the open window. The clouds were lifting.

"Black Jack."

"Are you sure?"

"Yes."

"I've got something for you." I hadn't noticed the book lying at his feet until he picked it up and handed it to me. It was bound in black leather and felt heavy in my hands.

"This was your father's. You know, there's not much to do on a boat at night, and he liked to write down his thoughts. There's all kinds of stuff in there about how happy he was when you were born, and lyrics to songs he liked, and even some recipes. Oh yeah, and jokes." I stared at it. "Take it. It's yours now."

I took the journal. In the gloom all I could tell was that it was Papa's writing, all right, with the same cramped letters he'd used on the note in my wallet.

"How did you end up with it?"

"He left it behind at the deli one day and when I tried to return it, he told me to keep it. I should have given it to you long ago."

Chester Street was not far from Lake Ontario. Maybe a five-minute walk, even at Mr. D.'s slow pace. I took my remaining bottle of Pepsi and poured it out. I folded up

Papa's little note and poked it into the bottle. Then I screwed the lid on and threw it in the lake.

I was done. "Let's go home," I said.

❦

That was five years ago. A lot of water has flowed under Montréal's bridges since then, but the good stuff, the Olympic Stadium, the smoked meat, and Mont-Royal are still there. I'm studying Political Science at McGill University. I still work for Mr. Deli on weekends, and at the Casino de Montréal on Thursday and Friday nights – I'm one of the croupiers at the poker table. That's how I pay my tuition. I still like the same music: U2, Nirvana, and Brel. Some things don't change, and won't ever change. Like Luc. Although he's growing up and will probably be taller than me, he'll always by my little brother. He's almost eleven years old now. Time goes by so fast.

❦

It hasn't been easy. There are very black days, but life is more powerful in the end than death. Papa made a tragic decision. He should not have given up on life.

When I miss Papa, I walk up to Mont-Royal, or I go up to the Saint-Joseph's Oratory. I imagine him right beside me, listening to what I have to tell him. To passersby I probably look like a nut who's talking to himself, but I don't care. It makes me feel good, like rolling down my car windows on a hot summer's night and singing along with the radio at the top of my lungs.

As for Maman, she left her office job to become a landscaper, so she can smell all the greenery she loves, especially the cedars and the pines. Sputnik's getting old now and he doesn't chase Frisbees, but he rides in the truck with Maman every day.

Houston works for his father's construction company. He likes to party a lot. I don't see him as often as I used to. Caroline took a year off, and went to work at Club Med somewhere in the Caribbean. They are the only ones who I still hear from. Jul went back to Ontario after that year, but I remember her, especially when I smell lily of the valley in the spring.

Aunt Sophie married George. Her wedding dress was green, like his hat and the pistachio cake. They spent weeks training Spaetzle to be the ring bearer. Luc and I were ushers. They've adopted two little red-haired boys.

～

When Luc turned eight, I taught him how to play poker. We made quite a ceremony of it. Maman cleared off the kitchen table, and we cracked open a new deck of cards.

"Fish is for kids. Now it's time to show you how the grown-ups play." I fanned the cards out expertly.

He watched, wordless, his cheeks full of popcorn. I could see myself in him, sitting at the table with Papa.

"Always hold your cards close to you, close to your heart. If you don't, the others can see them. If you get a good hand, tell yourself that you're lucky, but don't brag about it. It's what you do with your cards that counts."

I wanted to show Luc how to play his cards well, to tell him that cheating is never worth it, that life is beautiful, and royal straight flushes are rare, but exist for real. That life's a game, and enjoying it is okay. Laughing is just as important as being serious. Card games never last very long anyway. Nothing lasts forever, either.

ACKNOWLEDGMENTS

I would like to thank Tundra Books for their confidence: especially Kathy Lowinger, for her generosity and judicious advice.

Thanks to Michael Levine, who believes in me, and in my ideas. Thanks to Patrick Watson, for taking the time to read my manuscript, and also for his wise words that helped me to find a new perspective. Thanks to John Fraser for providing me a quiet place at Massey College for my writing. Thanks to Maxine Quigley for her patience and her smile.

Thanks to Ginette Chalifour, my mother, who's a model of courage, love, and integrity. Thanks to Mario Rondeau, my stepfather, for his patience and wisdom. Thanks to Yvonne Cantara, my aunt, for her kindness and her open-mindedness. Thanks to Mark Prior, and Luc Bernard for welcoming me into their family and for their generosity. Thanks to Julie Héroux, my friend since grade one, in whom I have the deepest confidence. Thanks to Françoise Pelletier for the help she provided me in my first years of teaching and Michelle Marcelin for the intelligence of her words and her wise advice.

I love you.